Mogollon Rim Rider

When he rode into the little trail town of Chico in North Arizona Territory, all Cassidy wanted was a bath, a decent meal and a glass of whiskey. What he got was a gunfight, a bank robbery and a price on his head for a crime he did not commit. Those who did commit it, though, had taken Cassidy's life savings with them.

But the ex soldier and army scout wouldn't let matters lie and soon he was on the retribution trail.

Lead would fly before justice was finally done.

By the same author

Apache Country
Carrigan's Claim

Mogollon Rim Rider

WALT MASTERSON

DORSET COUNTY COUNCIL	
Bertrams	04.02.07
	£11.25

© Christopher Kenworthy 2007
First published in Great Britain 2007

ISBN 978-0-7090-8227-9

Robert Hale Limited
Clerkenwell House
Clerkenwell Green
London EC1R 0HT

The right of Walt Masterson to be identified as
author of this work has been asserted by him
in accordance with the Copyright, Designs and
Patents Act 1988

Typeset by
Derek Doyle & Associates, Shaw Heath
Printed and bound in Great Britain by
Antony Rowe Limited, Wiltshire

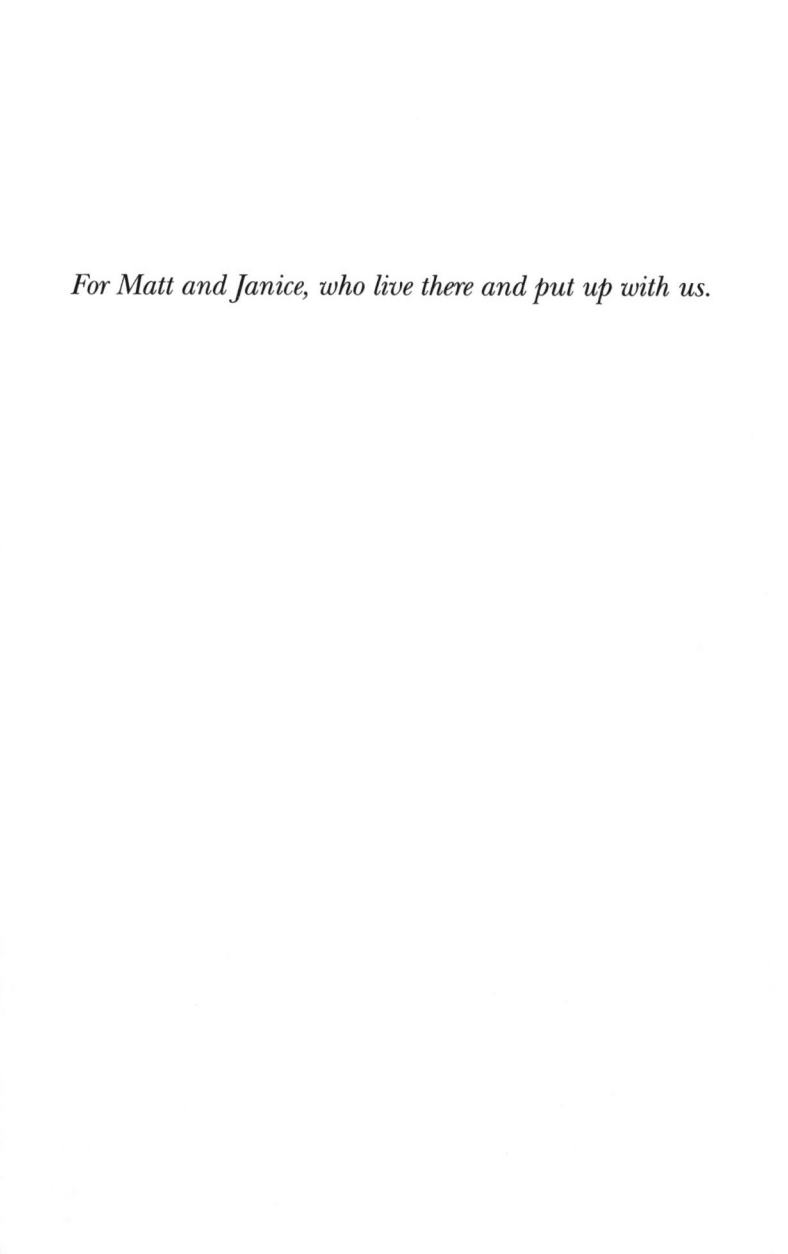

For Matt and Janice, who live there and put up with us.

CHAPTER ONE

The big bay was nervous coming down from the rim-rock, and as a result so was Cassidy. He rode with his reins loosely held in his left hand, his right on his thigh close to the butt of the Colt and his eyes restlessly examining the countryside under the shade of the wide, black hat.

The country, Cassidy reckoned, was worth the attention. The Mogollon Rim would make a man's breath come short in most places in the world, and Cassidy also reckoned he had been to most places in the world.

The Mogollons were a picture at this time of the year. Soaring cliffs, masses of green leaves just now shading into the rich tones of the autumn, with the gold of the cottonwoods down there on the flat land shading up to the rich reds of the maples.

Away, far, far away in the distance, he could see the loom of the White Mountains, and between him and them lay a huge stretch of green pines.

A scene to take a man's breath away, sure. But an Apache arrow would take his breath away just as quickly and a sight more permanently, so he rode carefully, stopping in the loom of the trees before risking the clearings, picking his own trail along game paths which did not follow obvious lines of least resistance.

Cassidy had good reason to be careful.

There were vengeful men on his trail, and a dead lawman back in the town they were beginning to call Chico. So he watched his back trail constantly.

Ahead of him, there were outlaws with watchful eyes and ready trigger-fingers and a bag of gold coins which by rights belonged to Cassidy. So he was equally wary of the trail ahead.

And then, of course, there were the Apache. It was not a time to stop and admire the scenery. But the bay needed a break, so he let it walk into a little cove halfway down the trail, where he could see the great spread of the Tonto Basin before him, loosened the saddle girth and let the horse feed on a bate of grain. He made coffee on a hatful of fire, and chewed jerky while he watched the land under his eye.

He had been a fool to stop at Chico, he knew that. Coming down from the frying heat of the Mohave desert, he had hungered after a plate of steak and potatoes he had not cooked himself, a glass of whiskey and a hand of cards.

Cassidy admitted even to himself he had a weakness for cards, so rather than take his saddle-bag full of money into the saloon with him, he had lodged it in the bank in the little adobe cube across the street. That money had been a long time earning, cost him two holes in his hide and a sword slash across his chest which had come close to opening him up and made him very leery of French cavalry troopers. He had carried the money and acquired the scars across a very long distance by avoiding the society of men who might take the cash off him.

He intended to turn the money into a little spread in the green valley he had found between the heights of the Superstitions, and raise horses there. Cassidy was fond of horses. He understood them and he thought they understood him. Also, they did not carry guns or knives, and they did not become protective about their womenfolk.

With his life savings locked in the bank's big, iron safe, he relaxed a bit. More than a bit, a lot.

He had his steak and potatoes and he had his whiskey, which was inevitably a disappointment, because in a town like Chico the whiskey was likely to be of local manufacture and include such ingredients as rattlesnake heads to give it bite, and a rat or two to give it body.

It was said of Taos Lightning whiskey that nobody who ever tasted it survived long enough to become an addict, and Chico's Lucky Strike Saloon's whiskey must have been a second cousin twice removed on the downhill side of the family, for it tasted worse.

The little town of Chico interested Cassidy. At one time in his life he had been a sheriff in just such a town, and he was fascinated by the resemblance between Sidewinder Flats and Chico. There was the same dirt street, facing on to which was the general store, which sold everything from miners' pickaxes to ribbons for ladies' finery.

There was a smattering of saloons, ranging from the Mexican cantina, all adobe arches and low doorways at the south end of town to the false front of the Lucky Strike. There was a restaurant, frequented no doubt by the ranchers' wives and daughters when they came in to buy the bolts of cloth and frills they made into surprisingly good dresses for the social occasions.

And there was the huddle of buildings tucked away behind the main street, like an anthill and connected by passageways and covert gaps in the adobe walls and fences between the back yards in which the majority of the poorer folk of Chico lived and depressingly often, died.

The main street was where the better off did their shopping, bought their stores and ate their steak and potatoes. The shanty town was where the worse off folk had their existences. Well-advised people stayed away from it during the hours of darkness and treated it with deep suspicion during the hours of daylight. Such caution paid off.

But it was the closest Cassidy had been to civilization, represented by a tin bath full of hot water, a rough cotton towel and a bed with sheets on it for many months, and he wanted to feel clean and well fed on food he had not shot, caught or trapped and cooked himself, mellow from a drink, and relaxed over cards.

He started his relaxation by buying himself a new outfit in the general store. The storekeeper tried to interest him in a broadcloth suit and a cotton shirt with a hangman's noose neck, and pleats in the breast, but he chose instead a dark-brown wool shirt, jeans, socks and a new union suit. His leather vest was an old friend and beside, had a secret pocket he had designed himself, and he stood himself a wide, flat black hat.

He added a few boxes of .44 bullets because they fitted both his Colt and his Winchester repeating rifle, and a new silk bandanna because it would serve several purposes, including keeping out dust, keeping his neck warm and protecting it from chafing against his collar, filtering drinking water, and serving as a sling if needed.

He felt smart and clean when he had dressed, and debated for a moment whether to put on his gun-belt. Surely, he thought, here in civilization he could go around without a sidearm. Then he thought back to Sidewinder Flats, checked the loads in the Colt, and slung it on his hip. He felt naked without its familiar weight, anyhow.

He changed his mind over sleeping in the hotel, too, when he threw back the blankets on the bed and saw a flea jump on the white of the sheets. In some months of sleeping rough on the road, he had somehow managed to get rid of the fleas he had picked up in his last town, and he wanted to stay that way.

Clean clothes, a clean skin and a clean bed he thought to himself, and decided to have his game of cards, his steak and his drink and then sleep outside town under a grove of cottonwoods he had noticed on the way in. There would be water down there, which would keep his horse happy, and a carpet of leaves which would act as a warning if anybody tried to creep up on him.

There was no way he could get his money out of the bank tonight, anyway, and he would have to come back for it in the morning.

So he brought his bedroll and his warbag down to the saloon, got his horse from the stables where it was just making itself comfortable for the night, and saddled it and stood it at the hitching rail outside the saloon.

Carrying his rifle and his saddle-bags he settled down inside the saloon and ordered his meal.

Sidewinder Flats had been just like this place, he thought as he ordered from the waitress and stretched his legs out under the table. All the equipment of civilization, without the finish.

Cassidy had been in London and Paris in his life, worn a red tunic and fought Afghans in the Khyber Pass, and Berbers in a dark-blue greatcoat in the Sahara. He had scouted for General Crook and gathered up horses for the US Cavalry in New Mexico.

He liked the West. It reminded him of the rocks and sand of Afghanistan and General Crook he respected as a commander with the wiles of an Apache and the stamina of an Afghan. The general rode a mule, and carried his equipment on pack animals, which meant he could go where the Apache went, instead of being held back by loaded wagons. Cassidy approved of a soldier who took advantage of his enemies' knowledge of the land.

His steak and fried potatoes arrived, and with it a shot of whiskey. He sipped at it carefully, coughed and blotted his streaming eyes on the end of his new neck scarf. Then he ordered a glass of beer. It was safer.

The steak and fried potatoes were remarkably good. He had grown tired of game over the past few weeks, though he knew that when he hit the trail again, he would enjoy it just as much.

Cassidy finished the meal with a slice of apple pie doused in cream, and sat back to nurse his coffee and survey the room.

His saddle-bags and rifle were in the corner behind him, and he was using the bedroll as a cushion, so he had all his possessions within his sight, which in a town like Chico counted for quite a lot.

The girls at the bar tempted him not at all, though all three of them eyed him with interest.

He was a good looking man, and now that he was shaved, bathed and well-dressed, would have interested any woman. They did not, however, interest him. He had nothing against bar girls as such, but this trio was a sorry lot, faces lined and drawn, and the paint sat garishly on their cheeks. One of them had almost no bosom at all, and her low-cut gown fell away from her breast bone like a badly wrapped bandage. The other two were tubby and had the dead eyes and hard voices of their profession.

At the bar there were also a dozen or so men, two were wearing broadcloth suits and he classified them as local businessmen. Half a dozen were cowhands in from the neighbouring ranches. They wore range clothes, clean but worn, and they all carried guns.

The remaining few men were professionals. Two sat at a table by themselves, with a bottle and two glasses. Like Cassidy they also had schooners of beer, and he noticed that the level in the bottle had not gone down since he came in, though from time to time, one of the men raised a whiskey glass to his lips and put it down again. The level did not go down in the glasses either.

They were pretending to drink, but were not doing so. What they wanted, then, was a reason to be in the bar without having to slow themselves down with the poisonous liquid in the whiskey bottle. None of the other men seemed to acknowledge them, so they were either not locals, or locals nobody liked or trusted.

'More coffee, mister?' He looked up into the eyes of the waitress. She was a totally different proposition from the bar girls: a fresh-faced redhead with freckles and green eyes. A dangerous combination, in Cassidy's experience, but a very attractive one.

'Sure would, ma'am,' he said. 'And a smoke, too. You have a good cheroot?'

'We have cheroots. Make your own mind up about the "good" bit,' she said, and the green eyes twinkled back at him.

'I'll take a chance,' he said returning the grin. She went away and was on her way back, when one of the men at the table opposite looked over at him. He was a thin, bony man with a cadaverous face and a heavy moustache.

Cassidy had been aware for some time that the man had been watching him covertly, and the attention made him nervous. He was not surprised when the man spoke.

'That your Winchester, mister?' the question was meant to sound casual, but Cassidy detected a hard edge to it, and his right hand, out of sight under the table, flicked the thong off the hammer of the Colt.

'Ain't nobody else's,' he said mildly.

'Looks familiar to me!' said the man loudly. The tone of voice attracted the attention of the men in the bar, as it was intended to. Heads started to turn.

'It's a Winchester,' said Cassidy. 'Maybe you seen another one, sometime. They look right similar.'

There was a mutter of laughter along the bar. The man flushed, and his eyes narrowed.

'You tryin' to make a fool out o' me?' he asked in a voice heavy with menace.

Cassidy picked up his coffee cup and took a drink before he answered. An observant man might have noticed that he handled the cup with his left hand and his right was under the table out of sight. A careful man might have drawn some conclusions from these two facts.

Moustache was neither observant nor careful. Worse, he was angry. What had started out as an attempt to buffalo a drifting cowhand, and maybe provoke him into an unequal fight, was not going his way.

He started to stand up from the table, and his companion, who seemed to be more observant, reached out to restrain him, only to be shrugged angrily off.

'You tryin' to make a fool o' me?' he snarled.

Cassidy gave him a friendly grin.

'Hell, no!' he said, putting down the cup. 'I couldn't possibly improve on the job you're doin' your own self!'

It took a second or two for the insult to sink in, then Moustache came up out of his chair with a roar of rage, reaching for his gun.

Cassidy stood up, kicking the table over, and exposing his own drawn Colt, hammer cocked and pointing straight between the troublemaker's eyes.

'Don't!' he said, once, flatly. The man froze ludicrously in mid-draw, his pistol just clear of the holster. Cassidy pointed at his still seated friend without taking his eyes off the gunman.

'You can keep your hands on the table, and live,' he told the man. 'Or you can die right here and now! Make up your own mind. I don't give a damn!'

The seated man carefully laid his empty hands on the tabletop.

'Good. You choose life,' Cassidy said. 'Now, you, Moustache! You seem all fired keen to make a fight with a man you never seen before! Now's your chance! You can drop that gun and live, or you can try to get me in the time it takes for a bullet to get from here to there. Think you're fast enough?'

He should have killed the man straight out, he knew, but he was unwilling to kill over such a stupid matter. Also he was curious to find out why the two seemed determined to provoke trouble. He was certain he had never seen either before they came into the saloon, and they were clearly there for a purpose. He doubted if it was because they wanted to kill him. That was incidental.

The steam had gone out of Moustache's rage. He stood like a statue, between fighting and giving in, and the tension in the room slowly eased.

'Open your hand and let it drop,' Cassidy told the would-be gunman. 'That's all you need to do, to live! Why die?'

The man's eyes flickered round the room and Cassidy could almost hear the wheels creaking around in his head. Finally, he admitted, even to himself, that he had no chance.

He opened his hand and the gun fell on the floor. It was not even cocked.

'Good!' Cassidy felt bitter. Gone was his relaxed evening in town, his game of cards and his good night's sleep. These two would never let this humiliation drop. He had, perhaps, only postponed the inevitable. But he had at least saved himself the trouble of a court hearing. And in front of a saloon full of witnesses.

'Now, get out!' he said. The seated man reached out for the gun on the floor, and Cassidy shook his head.

'Leave it! And yours! Take it out with your left hand, hold it by finger and thumb, drop it on the floor. Do it now!'

For a moment he thought the man would try something, but after a short pause, he followed the instruction. The waitress came unstuck from her frozen position at the bar, and the rest of the people in the room began to move again with a murmur of a conversation.

Cassidy gestured at the door.

'Out!' He said. 'If I see you again, anyplace, any time, I'll start to shooting! That's an Irish promise!'

CHAPTER TWO

The atmosphere in the saloon was thick enough to saddle a horse. Cassidy grimaced and picked up the dropped gun from the floor, holstered his own and walked to the bar. He collected the second weapon on the way, and unloaded both. He pocketed the bullets.

'I'll leave these with you,' he told the barkeep, laying them flat in the polished surface. 'If they don't come back, give them to the sheriff.'

'And if they do?' said the barkeep, who was a thickset, bald man in a fancy vest and long apron.

'Why, return them to their owners,' said Cassidy. 'What else?'

'You better keep them your own self,' said a thin man in working clothes who was sitting at a table across the room. 'Know who them two are?'

'Sure. They're two men think they're bad because they can try to buffalo a stranger in a bar,' said Cassidy. 'They may live long enough to learn better, but I wouldn't bet on it.'

'Them two,' said the thin man with the air of a messenger imparting grave news, 'Them two is the McGibbon brothers, that's who!'

Cassidy assumed an expression of interested awe.

'That so? The McGibbon brothers? *The* McGibbon brothers?'

'Sure are,' said the thin man with a smirk. 'Now you see what you done?'

'Sure do! I took the guns off of two men who think they're tough. You a friend of theirs?'

The thin man looked shifty. 'Know them,' he said, 'seen 'em around.'

'Well, if you see 'em around again,' said Cassidy, 'tell 'em where their guns are at!'

He pushed through the batwing doors, and instantly dropped to one knee. Out in the darkness of the street, two guns banged out, and the doors smacked open again and started swinging as though they were alive.

Cassidy fired back at where the muzzle flashes had been, and was rewarded with a yelp of pain. He rolled over until he was behind the water trough by the hitching rail, and peered round it. His ears were ringing with his own shots, but out in the dark, he could hear muffled voices and then the sound of feet retreating.

He waited until the sound faded and got up, cautiously. Someone had furnished the ambushers with replacement guns, and that right quickly. That meant they had friends somewhere in town. Nobody, he noticed, had come out of the saloon to see what happened.

Cassidy put his saddle-bags over his horse's back, and secured them to the saddle. Then he led the horse across the street, walking on the saloon side of the animal, and struck a match as he hunkered down to examine the ground.

There were drops of blood near the corner of the building across the street, and fresh tracks in the dust. He examined them carefully. One man – the wounded one from the way the drops overlaid his tracks – wore square-toed, high-heeled boots, and the other riding boots with narrow soles and a pointed toe. There was a pronounced amount of wear on the right heel, which suggested he walked with a limp, and Cassidy recalled that when they left the saloon, one of them had limped slightly.

He had been in the same place for too long and he let the match die. He would know their tracks again. But he still did not know why they had chosen to make trouble for him.

Simple bullying of a stranger was unlikely in a town like Chico, where strangers passing through would tend to be tough, cross-grained men not easy to dominate. Yet there had been a reason for the trouble seeking, and he would dearly love to know what it was.

At the moment, though, he needed a campsite somewhere out of town, and sheltered from the night wind and curious eyes. He swung into the saddle, and clicked his tongue at the horse. The bay stepped out willingly enough, and Cassidy let him find his own way down the road.

He found the campsite he had been seeking a mile or so down the trail. There was a stand of cottonwoods which indicated water, and an outcropping of rocks alongside it which made an ideal miniature fort. Leaving the horse picketed nearby to disturb him if anybody approached, he made a dry camp without a fire, rolled himself in his blankets and after thoroughly stamping around the little basin in the rocks to make sure there were no rattlesnakes in it, laid his head on his saddle, his Winchester alongside his blankets and fell into the light sleep of the experienced Indian fighter.

He was awakened by the horse, which was moving nervously around the little basin. He lay for a long moment, listening, and was about to roll over and go back to sleep when he heard the sound which had roused the animal.

It was about a half an hour before dawn, he reckoned. The sky was very dark away towards the west, but there was already a suggestion of dove grey to the east, and the sun would be up shortly.

In the soft light, he tapped out his boots in case a tarantula or a scorpion had sought shelter in them in the dark, and pulled them on, before cautiously peering around the cottonwood grove over his natural battlements.

All seemed to be peaceful, and he was turning away to saddle the horse when he heard the slightest suggestion of movement over towards the base of one of the trees.

The ground was wet, there, and it looked as though there might be water under the earth for the digging of a hole. Maybe a underground tributary of the springs which had given Chico its reason for being there.

In case he had to move fast, he got the saddle on the bay and pulled the cinches up twice. The horse made a dummy snap at him and he punched its belly to make sure it had not inflated itself to keep the cinch loose. The dun breathed out, and he pulled the cinch up to the usual notch, and fondled the horse's nose.

All the time, he was listening carefully, but he got the horse saddled and ready before he investigated further. Holding its lead rein, he led out of the little hollow and down towards the cottonwood grove.

He found the wounded man at once, because he had left a drag mark from the road to the grove. He was lying face down just within the cottonwoods, unconscious. His clothes were unremarkable range equipment: jeans and a flannel shirt, riding boots, with large rowelled spurs, a gun-belt which held only a few cartridges, and a leather and canvas vest. He was hatless, and the bandanna had been taken from his neck and wrapped tightly round his thigh. It had done nothing to stem the blood which was oozing through it.

Cassidy leaned down and turned the man over. The eyes stayed closed, but Cassidy knew the type. A hard face with high cheekbones, a hawk nose and slit of a mouth. A harsh face, and now, a dying one. Cassidy had seen that cheesy pallor before, and it indicated a dramatic loss of blood.

He checked both hands and the holster on the worn gunbelt, and found no sign of a weapon. The man must have dropped it on his desperate drag from the road, if not before. The bullet which had hit him had entered from behind, and was still in the wound, high on the inside of his thigh. There was no exit wound at the front.

It would need a clever surgeon and a hospital to get it out and so far as Cassidy knew, there was neither doctor nor hospital within a hundred miles.

Effectively the man was dead, though his fluttering breathing denied it.

Cassidy made him as comfortable as he could. He was reaching for his saddle-bags when he heard hoofs on the road, and straightened up, sliding the Winchester out of its case on the saddle.

He stood behind the horse and watched the road, and could see a group of men coming along in the growing light. They were riding slowly and checking the road and the roadside for tracks. A posse, Cassidy guessed, seeking the wounded man.

And the wounded man was here, with Cassidy. Being treated for his wounds, and tended in a camp in the cottonwoods.

A situation which might easily be misunderstood.

MOGOLLON RIM RIDER

*

The posse, to a man, misunderstood it. They followed the wounded man's tracks, and the tracks led them to Cassidy. For most of them, that was enough.

They pulled up in a bunch, and looked over Cassidy and the wounded man, who was lying on his side, and had been bandaged. One man started to move his horse to the side, and Cassidy said:

'Stay right where you are, fella! We got things to discuss, here, and I ain't got time to pussy-foot around!'

The rider stopped. Cassidy sounded like he meant what he said, and in any case the posse, bunched, could only see his head above his saddle and his legs below it. It would be a lucky shooter who managed to get his gun out, take the difficult shot at head or legs, and survive the pointed Winchester.

'Now,' said Cassidy. 'Here's the deal. I'll tell you guys just the once, and that's all. You listenin'?'

Not a man spoke, but the barrel of the Winchester held all their eyes. One man, who was able to tear his eyes away from it, said in a surprised whisper: 'Hell, that's the guy braced the McGibbons in the bar last night!'

There was a ripple of surprised interest and recognition. Cassidy swore to himself.

'Yeah,' said Cassidy. 'And not one of you moved a hand to help out! I ain't in love with your town, neither! So listen close!'

The posse remained like rocks in the saddle. Not a man of them did not remember the speed of the draw with which he had disarmed the town roughs, or the accuracy of his shooting when ambushed outside the saloon.

'Keep your hand off that gun, Zeke!' said one of them in a stage whisper. 'He hit Al McGibbon plumb centre in the dark across the street – and they shot first!'

The posse remained still.

'Yeah, and I had to come out here to camp overnight. Thanks a bunch, fellas!' he snarled. 'Now, you bring trouble to me! I found this here guy tryin' for the spring an hour ago. He's been shot from behind, and I don't think he's going to make it.'

There was a ripple of interest.

'Now, I got business in that bank of yourn, back in town, and when I'm through with that, I aim to make tracks. You got business with this guy, you better hurry because he ain't goin' to be around for long, from the sound of his breathin'.'

He raised one foot and put his boot in the stirrup. 'In the meantime, I'm going back to town to that there bank. Don't be stupid enough to follow me.'

There was a murmur from among the group. One of them started to say something, and the man next to him hushed him. But the men were too keyed up to keep quiet.

'Won't do you no good holding up the bank!' said the tail-ender who had tried to move his horse. 'It's plumb empty!'

'What?'

'Bunch of guys broke in last night while we was in the saloon watching your play actin' with the McGibbons and broke open the safe,' said the talkative one. 'Cleaned it out and escaped, came right this way! We got him on the run, and looks like he made it this far all by himself.'

'Or maybe not!' shouted one of the others. 'Maybe he was met by the lookout! Maybe you brung him this way to lie up, and didn't expect us to catch up so soon!'

There was a rumble of agreement. The posse had started out late, and seemed to have lost track of the safe-breaking gang, and they were loath to let this chance to make someone pay slip through their hands. They had a rope and at least one victim.

'Come on, he can only get one or two! Let's rush him!' shouted a voice from the back of the group. Men who thought up bright ideas like rushing an armed marksman usually were at the back of the group, Cassidy had noticed.

'Sure, rush me!' he said. 'You lead 'em, loud mouth! Come on! Right to the front, where I can see you!'

The men at the front of the posse seemed in favour of that idea. Most of them started looking over their shoulders, and none made any attempt to move forward.

Cassidy swung his leg over the saddle while they were arguing among themselves. One of the posse saw him do it, and shouted a warning, at the same time grabbing for his pistol. It went off as he pulled it from the holster, and his horse, startled, started to buck madly, throwing the whole tightly packed group of horsemen into disarray.

Cassidy looked down at the bank robber. The man had made an attempt to turn on to his back, and apparently died in the act of doing it. At any rate, he was now lying in a bloodstained heap. His eyes were open and glazing and blood had run from his wound to drench his jeans.

All this Cassidy took in as he clapped his heels to the bay's flanks, and hung on while the horse, already made skittish by the turmoil, went off like a race-winner.

Cassidy steered him through the cottonwood, and over the slight rise behind them, on to a low valley leading to the south and east, and let him run. The big horse, rested and watered, settled into a distance eating stride, and allowed himself after the initial burst of speed to be brought down to an easy gait.

Cassidy was broke again, he was on the run, and he was heading for Apache territory at a time when even General Crook needed a regiment to go into it.

The luck of the Irish, he told himself. But the idea did not raise the grin it usually managed to do.

He was mad through and through, and if his luck demanded a war party of Tonto Apaches, bring 'em on.

CHAPTER THREE

They followed, of course. Cassidy had been expecting it, because he expected that the money in the pip-squeak bank was all the town and the surrounding land possessed.

He reckoned that the bank had been robbed in the few hours since he left town, and before dawn. Probably when the McGibbon brothers had braced him in the saloon. He could think of no other reason for them to pick on him and a gunfight with a stranger passing through would be just the kind of thing to focus the population's attention on the saloon while there was mayhem going on elsewhere in the town.

Which meant that the McGibbons were involved in the bank robbery, which in turn meant that they would know where the robbers had gone, eventually. From his own knowledge of the northern part of Arizona Territory, he reckoned they would head for the Mogollon Rim which was a little to the south and away to the east. It would have several attractions for the robbers.

For one thing, the Mogollon Rim was a natural shelf of rock which slashed across the Territory from southeast to northwest. It was backed on the northern side by the Mogollon Plateau which was over a thousand feet higher than the Tonto Basin which nestled to the south of the Rim. Because of the sharp contrast between the lower, hotter basin to the south of the Rim, and the cooler land to the north, the long, precipitous scarp face made a natural barrier.

There were several ways through it, of course, and they were used enthusiastically by the Tonto Apache to raid north and flee south when the Army came after them in the basin.

General Crook, for whom Cassidy had regularly scouted and for whom he had a considerable respect, was based at what was now called Fort Verde, where the Verde river ran past some old cliff dwellings in a deep cut, and went off towards the west.

Crook had also established a base at Fort Apache in the White Mountains to the south and east, among the less troublesome White Mountain Apache, who sullenly accepted his presence.

The Apache had a reluctant respect for Crook because he was clever enough to use their own tactics against them. Where other commanders toiled along hampered by their equipment and wagons full of the impedimenta of modern military hardware, Crook used mules. Just mules. He even rode one himself in preference to a horse.

If he could not carry any article of his equipment on a mule train, then he left it behind. He reduced his men's equipment to a manageable minimum, laid a heavy emphasis on knowledge of the local district and its demands and drawbacks.

The Apache warriors, magnificent guerrilla fighters that they were, had become used to escaping their Army pursuers by travelling light and fast and taking to broken high ground with narrow rocky defiles, where the Army's artillery and heavy equipment wagons could not follow. Crook developed an army band which was lightly equipped and heavily armed and as agile as the Apache.

He even managed to get mountain guns which were carried on mules, and disconcerted the Apache who had grown used to rifles and six shooting pistols – had in fact grown expert in their use – but had not until now come up against artillery.

'We were doing fine until you started shooting wagons at us!' one Apache chieftain complained in disgust.

Crook's troopers were guided by scouts recruited among the Apache themselves, and they learned from them.

The Apache were startled to find themselves pushed further and harder than they had ever been before, and they reacted first with astonishment and then with renewed venom.

All that was by the way at the moment, for Cassidy. Finding the bank robbers and recovering his money was his first priority. But there were others.

First was avoiding the posse. He thought he had thrown it off more than once, only to find it emerging from a stand of trees back along his trail, or see its cooking fire in the darkness.

Now, he topped out on the edge of the Rim and looked back. Sure enough, there was a faint mist of dust back there, which meant that the dogged pursuit was continuing. He swore bitterly. So far he had avoided killing anybody, which meant that when he finally managed to get back to his original purpose, he could at least protest to the authorities. Since the main authority round here was General Crook, he knew he would have a sympathetic hearing.

He leaned down from the saddle and examined the trail he had been following. The tracks were by now familiar to him, there were six in the gang, one of them riding a horse with a deformed hoof which needed a slightly oddly shaped shoe, and one riding a horse which must be huge. Its tracks were driven deep where there was soft ground, and it had feet like soup plates.

They were the last horses to pass down this trail and since he had picked them up just outside Chico, and found them time and time again on his flight from the posse, he was pretty certain these were the tracks of the bank raiders. And now, from the posse's point of view, his tracks were with the bank raiders', and that was in itself doubly incriminating.

The view over the Tonto Basin showed him trees and the light yellow of the cottonwoods which followed the river's course, but little else. There was no smoke to indicate cooking fires or settlements, nothing to show it was anything but a sleeping forest. But it was not, and Cassidy knew it better than anybody.

And of course the Indians. In the White Mountains to the east, there were Apaches. The White Mountain Apaches were reputed not to be as aggressive as the Chiricahua to the south, the Mascaleros in New Mexico, or the Mimbres. The Tonto basin had its own breed, the Tonto Apache.

He clicked his tongue and the horse continued on its downward trail, picking its way as delicately as a dancer, and Cassidy let it get on with its business undisrupted and concentrated instead on watching for Indian sign.

Somewhere down there, under the canopy of trees there were several people Cassidy was desperate to find, and far more than several of the people he was desperate not to find. The latter of course were all Indians and Cassidy was not silly enough to believe that the Indian had not detected him. He rode loose in the saddle, with his carbine across his knees.

The horse was already entering the trees when he heard the crackle of distant gunfire.

Under normal circumstances, he would have turned his horse's head away from it, but where there was gunfire there was likely to be white men and Indians, and the white men he was seeking were the most likely ones in this setting.

Cautiously, he turned the horse's head towards

it and even more cautiously, he picked his way along the faint trail which wound among the trees. There were fresh hoof-prints, where the ground was soft enough, and they were of shod horses, which meant they were ridden by white men.

Where the shooting was, there too would be his money, and Cassidy was determined to have it.

He pushed the horse along as fast as he dared, but before he could come up on the scene of the firing, it had stopped.

Cassidy slowed immediately and let the horse pick its own wary pace. Somewhere up ahead were the men who had stolen his money and a group of unknown size which was most probably Apaches. There was also the posse to account for and Cassidy honestly did not know where they were, but suspected the Indians would settle that worry for him.

The thought reminded him that they might also settle Cassidy, and he slowed his pace even further, riding a little forward on the saddle, and then stopping to listen.

He heard another shot, which puzzled him. If the Apache had been victorious, he ought by now to be hearing their yells of satisfaction. If not, surely the firing would be resumed.

Under the trees he came across the first dead

man. He was lying face down, half hidden from sight by the brown grass under the trees, one arm stretched out in front of him and a tuft of the brown, sere grass clutched in his extended hand. His horse had run on a few paces before it had stopped to crop the grass. It looked tired and dejected and had plainly been ridden hard.

Cassidy examined the surrounding trees without finding anything sinister. The pursuing Indians, presumably, had simply left the horse for attention later and carried on after the fleeing white men.

Cassidy took the dead man's pistol and brand new Winchester to prevent the Indians from snatching them up, made sure they were loaded and pushed the pistol into his belt and the rifle into his saddle scabbard. With his own rifle and pistol in reserve, it gave him formidable firepower, and deprived the Indians of extra weapons. The dead man's weapons were fully loaded and he had a few rounds in the loops on his belt, but not many. The rifle needed cleaning, too.

Re-mounting his horse, he was about to push on, when it occurred to him to try and establish the dead man's identity.

CHAPTER FOUR

He dismounted again, and searched the dead man's pockets. They yielded up surprisingly little for a man who presumably was a successful bank robber. A used square of cotton handkerchief, and bandanna – surprisingly, of silk – a purse with a drawstring which contained half a dozen coins of low value and two golden eagles, which Cassidy pocketed in pathetically little recompense for his stolen savings, a worn Bowie knife and a Barlow knife which had been sharpened almost down to a thread.

There was a small packet of letters from a girl called Dallas, which he wrapped in the silk scarf and put in his saddle-bag to return to her when he got to a town once again, and a ball of string. In his saddle-bags were a skillet, a water bottle with a dent in it, a couple of worn shirts and a spare union suit which had been darned on the buttocks more than once, and which Cassidy returned to the saddle-bags. The Indians, he reflected, were welcome to the rest of the meagre belongings.

He climbed on to his horse again, tipped his hat to the dead bank robber and sent the big bay cautiously along the trail ahead. The dead man's horse made no attempt to run away from him, and Cassidy gathered up its trailing rein and took the animal along with him.

He found the second dead man within a hundred yards. The bandit had not died as easily as the first. He was lying on his back beside the trail, his spine arched in his final death agony and his face contorted with pain, which was hardly surprising because he had been disembowelled.

There was no point in hoping that he had been already dead when that had happened, because the Indians would not have bothered if he had been.

His horse was lying by the trail beside its owner, a bullet through its head, which explained how he had been brought down. His saddle-bags had been emptied contemptuously over his body, and contained no more than the first man. Whoever headed this gang seemed to have carried the spoils himself, and taken them with him. Since Cassidy knew there were now only four of them because the citizens of Chico had seen six of them emerge from the bank, that left four more up ahead.

As he came to that conclusion there was a small spatter of firing to confirm it. A static fight, then, in the pines. Cassidy quickened his pace to a lope until a couple of shots dead ahead brought him to a standstill. The led horse stopped behind the bay and gave Cassidy a chance to get down off the horse and scout ahead.

The tale was written in the trail. The white men were mounted on horses whose gait betrayed their exhaustion. The chase would not last much longer, and as Cassidy came to this conclusion, a spatter of shots from ahead told him he was right.

He ground-hitched the horses and pushed on through the trees until he came to a huge pile of tumbled boulders forming a natural fortress in a clearing. Ahead there was open ground.

He located the Indians almost immediately. They had found themselves a series of firing places, and the two on the right were keeping up a searching fire among the boulders, which from his point of view, another warrior could be seen inching his way through the natural spaces and up the boulder pile. None of the defenders' shots were directed towards his position, so the quarry was obviously not aware of his approach. It was slow, but the more deadly because it was unobserved and apparently unsuspected.

Cassidy estimated the number of Indians at three or four, and cursed under his breath. He was going to have to expose his presence to a substantial war party which was currently not aware of him.

However even if he were inclined to abandon white men to the fate which usually followed capture by Apaches, he had to recover the money, and the white men apparently had it.

He settled himself in a natural hollow between two of the rocks on the level and surveyed the slope carefully. There was at least one Indian on the left undetected and a further two or three in the firing party.

The dangerous one was the one on the left, because he was making a slow but steady process to outflank the defenders among the rocks.

He watched the warrior climb for a few seconds to make sure there were no more, then licked his thumb and wet the rear of the foresight on one of the Winchesters. The tiny glint of reflected sunlight on the bead emphasised it against the dark of the rocks, and he swung the rifle experimentally to practise his arc of fire, and then drew in a deep breath and let it trickle out while the sights lined up on the Apache close to the top, and squeezed the trigger steadily until the rifle kicked his shoulder.

The black powder smoke formed a cloud in the still air, and he immediately rolled out of the trench to his left and rose to one knee before seeking the Indians on the right.

His sight was empty and the hillside devoid of Apaches. He dropped immediately and heard a slug ricochet off the top of the rock.

Time to go. Cassidy crawfished backwards without raising his head from the ground level and when he was able, moved sideways along the foot of the rock pile.

Two more bullets spanged off the rocks where he had been, and he found himself opposite a kind of natural gully among the rocks, and crawled up it as fast as he could, taking up a new firing position among a minor rock pile which lifted his point of observation.

Almost immediately, he could see two Indians. They were tucked into a gap between the rocks, and looking back down the slope to his previous firing position. Their skin was the colour of the dust, and the cloths tied round their heads were ragged and faded to a sad brown shade. He could not see them until one of them moved to signal to his comrade which in turn provoked the comrade into signalling back.

Cassidy was taking up aim in the nearer of the two when another Indian moved, directly in front of him, and as the Winchester kicked against Cassidy's shoulder, the startled Apache gave a yelp of surprise and vanished again among the rock. The two Cassidy had been aiming at vanished immediately, and a shot spat rock splinters into his face.

Dabbing furiously at his stinging cheek, Cassidy dropped out of sight and moved as quickly as he could among the rocks. Above him in the pile a couple of shots rang out and there was the unmistakable sound of a bullet hitting human flesh nearby.

Cassidy dropped again, into a trough between rocks, rolled on his back just in time to see the outline of an Apache coming over the rocks towards him. He dropped the Winchester, pulled the Colt from his belt and shot the man as he fell into the trench beside him.

The falling warrior pinned him down, and Cassidy was already fighting with him when he realized the weight on him was inert. He was fighting off a dead man.

Frantically, he threw the corpse off him, just in time to see a second warrior vaulting over the rocks on the uphill side. As the man cleared the rock, there was a meaty slap followed instantly by the hollow boom of a rifle and blood sprayed from the side of his head. The body which hit the rocks was already dead.

Cassidy had just time to swear in surprised admiration – the shot had been remarkable and was obviously intentional – when there was another spatter of firing from further over on the rock pile, and the sound of receding hoof-beats punctuated by mocking yells.

Silence fell, and in the first seconds of the unnatural stillness, he clearly heard the blood dripping from the shattered head of the last Indian to die.

He collected both of his rifles from the bottom of the little trench, and slowly and with infinite caution, placed his hat on the muzzle of one of the rifles and raised it above the edge of the trench.

Nothing happened. He withdrew it, clambered over the bodies of the two Indians, and took a cautious peep round a rock. A broken vista of rocks and boulders devoid of life stretched up to the top of the little knoll. There was nothing but rock in sight.

'Sing out if you're still alive!' he called.

'I'm still alive!' replied a cautious voice. 'Are you hurt?'

He sat, silent, for a moment. The voice was a woman's voice, and it had an English accent. An upper-class English accent, at that. There was money and breeding in that voice, centuries of it.

It was the privilege and the unconscious superiority of voices like that which had driven him out of the British Army and out of India, to seek his fortune in America, and the west of America at that, where he met a different kind of Indian. Different but just as deadly. And a different kind of white man, too, if it came to that.

'Are you hurt?' he called, still examining the rocks in the direction of the voice for signs of Apaches who might have stayed behind when their comrades so noisily and obviously departed. Too obviously, he decided.

'Stay where you are and keep down!' he called. 'I'll make sure they are gone!'

He rolled over the next ridge of rock, and scouted the area carefully, though without success. The Apache were either gone, or too well hidden for him to find them, so he stood up quickly put a hand on the ridge of rock in front of him, and vaulted over it, dropping into the gap beyond.

There was neither a triumphant yell nor the scorching impact of a bullet. He repeated the manoeuvre with the same result, and repeated it yet again.

Nothing. The warriors were gone, it seemed. By this time he was several jumps nearer to where he reckoned she would be, and he made his way cautiously towards her, calling softly as he went.

She was sitting in a natural trench in the rocky ridge, unnaturally still and not touching a weapon that he could see, and pointedly not looking at him. When he got close enough, she said quietly but clearly, 'Behind the pointed rock on the left. Don't miss!'

He was startled but not paralysed when an Apache stood up from behind her, and threw a knife. Unable to dodge because he was in a narrow cleft in the rocks, he took the knife blade on the butt of one of the Winchesters.

The weapons dropped from his hand and he drew the Colt and fired in the same movement as the Indian dived over the rock.

The woman vanished. Cassidy fell forward behind the rock on his left and found himself looking at the soles of a pair of worn riding boots between two rocks. They were motionless and he swore bitterly that he had come too late.

'My pleasure in hearing proof that you are still alive is mitigated in part by the profanity of your language!' said the cut glass English voice acidly from the next hidey-hole.

'Sorry, ma'am!' said Cassidy, annoyed more at the fact that he had given her a chance to put him in his place than at the reproof. 'Next time I'll save your life in Oxford English. Suit you better?'

'Considerably, though Father was a Cambridge man!' she replied, cool as a glacier.

She sat up and gave Cassidy his second shock of the day.

He had been expecting a sun-toughened stringy English milady with skin like tanned leather and teeth like a horse, and he found himself facing one of the most beautiful women he had ever seen. She was remarkable, though not in the conventional fashion.

Her face was tanned all right, and she was no schoolgirl. Her jaw was strong, and her nose Grecian and straight. She was wide across the cheekbones and the eyes which regarded him under arched, dark brows were a deep hazel colour. Her hair was lustrous black and tied in a knot at the nape of her neck.

She had on a faded khaki shirt, open at the neck, and pulled in tightly at the waist with a man's wide, leather belt fastened with a big brass buckle, and supporting a flapped holster on her left hip and facing forwards. Her skirt was dark blue and full and covered in dust. There was a felt man's hat hanging between her shoulder blades on a thong.

Even her rifle was remarkable. It was lever-action and custom built with a telescopic sight mounted above the breech. A cumbersome weapon for a woman, particularly in these rocks, and yet she had killed and killed swiftly with it when required.

She was also pointing it at him now. He swallowed hard and hoped it was not on a hair trigger.

'I'm Cash Cassidy,' he said hoarsely, 'and I'd kinda like to stay that way, so I'd be obliged if you'll point that-thar cannon someplace else, ma'am. Carefully, too!'

She grinned and nodded.

'I'm Sarah Fennell. Deeply relieved to meet you, Mr Cassidy.

'Don't be frightened about the rifle. It only goes off when I want it to,' she said. But she raised the muzzle into the air and rested the butt on her knee. Cassidy's stomach muscles relaxed considerably and he breathed out in a long, slow movement.

Cassidy felt a sense of unreality stealing over him.

'Ma'am,' he said carefully, watching the rocks around them. 'We may have killed the man they left behind but they may not have gone far, and there's no tellin' when they'll take a fancy to comin' back.

'Apaches is fanciful folk. We'd best make tracks.'

She glanced at him and leaned forward and out of his line of sight to reappear a second later with the strap of a pack looped over her left shoulder and the rifle held in her right hand.

'Lead on, Macduff!' she said brightly. 'They took my horse, so you'll have to ride double. Unless you want to play the gentleman and walk.'

Cassidy recovered both his rifles and took a long look around the rocks before he hitched himself over the edge of the little dip and led her towards his horses.

'Last time I walked on a journey, ma'am, I had two thousand men with me and I was wearing a red coat,' he said. 'I didn't like it then, and I sure don't reckon I'd like it now. Even if I wasn't wearin' ridin' boots!'

All the same, he was glad to find both his horses were waiting for them when they threaded their way through the trees and away from the rocks. She had about her a certain steely quality which suggested to Cassidy that what Sarah wanted,

Sarah generally got.

She might well have to moderate her views in the coming few days, he told himself. Sarah had feet just as serviceable as his own.

CHAPTER FIVE

The horses greeted them with soft whickers and snuffles, and the new recruit even seemed to take to Sarah, so he handed her the reins and watched while she tied her pack behind the saddle where the late owner's bedroll was still stowed, and put her foot in the big stirrup.

When she threw her leg over the saddle, he noticed that under the long skirt, she was wearing what looked like men's jeans. At any rate, she rode astride the saddle with her skirts shaken down over her legs.

His first task was to find the tracks of the fleeing bandits, and he did so within half an hour. They had set off steadily east, and the Apaches had later found the tracks and followed them. That put them between Cassidy and his money and having a good looking woman with him – any woman at all, from the Apaches' point of view – doubled his jeopardy. When they realized he had Sarah in tow, they would find her a more potent attraction even than the chance to kill white men. And Sarah and Cassidy together provided the Indians with both.

Together the two of them followed the Apaches who in turn were following the fleeing bandits. In normal circumstances, Cassidy would have made tracks instantly in the opposite direction, but he was determined not to let his money ride away from him, and the money was the other side of the Indians, so he pressed on cautiously.

'How did you come across the Apache?' he asked the woman as they threaded their way through the trees.

'I didn't. They came across me,' she said. 'I left my horse and climbed into the rocks to fill my canteen at the spring up there, and then the white men came up riding like madmen, and shortly after them, the Indians.

'I heard some shooting when they got close and I knew what that meant, so I was trying to lie low but I saw them taking my horse, and I knew that my chances on foot and alone were pretty slender, so I shot the man who was taking the horse and they fell on me like a ton of bricks.'

He grunted. Something had happened to the tracks he was following and he was puzzled. The Indians' tracks led off to the north while the men he was also tracking held to their easterly heading.

It was not like Apache to be distracted, particularly on a murder raid which they clearly were, so what could have taken their attention quite so suddenly? He reached out a warning hand, and stopped Sarah as she was about to overtake him.

She started to make a surprised objection and then shut up and let him pull her horse to a standstill next to his. He leaned over from the saddle and whispered in her ear.

'I reckon they know we're behind them!' he hissed.

She nodded. 'I think I can see one,' she breathed back. 'He's in the tree over to the left, where my rifle is pointing. Shall I shoot him?'

He was surprised at her acute vision. He had seen the warrior himself only a second or so before, and the man was well hidden.

On the other hand, the warrior might be one of several in ambush. He allowed himself a careful survey of the surroundings but could not see any other warriors. But then, he wouldn't if they were in ambush.

He came to a decision almost as soon as the

Apaches did. Grabbing Sarah's reins, he kicked his horse into action and as they leapt forward, two arrows passed through the air where they had been and a third thumped into his saddle-bag.

He raced forwards amid a crackle of gunfire and felt a terrific blow low on his side and a hot gush of blood over his hip. Sarah gave an outraged bellow, and he heard her rifle bang like a howitzer.

Suddenly they were running free, with the Indians behind them and only open hillside in front. The trees had fallen away and open ground lay ahead, broken with rocks and leading back into the hills of the Rim.

The horses were breathing heavily and Cassidy slowed their headlong flight into an easy, ground-eating canter.

Far ahead along the line of the Rim he could see a notch which offered shelter and he headed them for it, keeping his hand clamped over the pad of silk on his hip. Sarah fell in behind him and after a moment he heard her startled gasp. He glanced down at his leg and saw that the blood from his wound had soaked down the side of his leg despite everything he could do. He had to stop and attend to the wound, and that right soon.

A little while later the hairline trail widened as it ran under a bulging overhang, that all but closed above the trail and he saw a darker patch of bush and creeper in the cliff side. The bay turned into the little cove formed there, and he found himself peering into a cave mouth. The horse shouldered into the entrance of its own accord, and stopped.

Cassidy began to turn towards Sarah to tell her to pull her mount in behind his own, but as he did so, his head started to spin, and the last thing he recalled was her cry of alarm.

There was the sound of bubbling water when he awakened, and he felt as though a horse had kicked him above the hip. He moved, and it felt as though the horse had done it again. He grunted and fell back and heard Sarah say: 'Keep still, you stupid man! I've nearly got you sewn up, and you try to tear it open again!'

He swore under his breath and raised just his head to find that he was lying on his back on a pile of pine needles and blankets, and that he had no trousers on and one leg of his union suit was cut off.

He gave a yelp of dismay and grabbed for the blanket to cover himself, and found his hand grabbed with fingers which seemed to have been reinforced with sprung steel.

'Keep still, dammit!' Sara hissed. 'And for pity's

sake, keep quiet. There are Indians around.' He froze instantly and fumbled for his gun, only to have it put into his hand. Sarah was leaning over him, and in her hand was a revolver which looked far too big for her.

She was looking towards the far side of the cave, and apparently ready for anything. 'You will burst the stitches I have managed to get in!' she warned him. 'Then I'll have to start again and it will take twice the time. Lie back and let me finish.'

She worked for a while, then slapped him on the hip. 'Stop moaning!' she said. 'You're done! Now a cup of coffee and some soup and you can get in a good night's sleep. Tomorrow we can push on!'

'Tomorrow be damned!' he said struggling upright, and swearing under his breath at the cat's-claw twitch of the stitching. 'Those boys have got my money, and I ain't gonna face the whole Apache nation for it. We got to get to them road agents before Geronimo and his boys!' He heaved himself on to his elbow, a surprisingly hard job. 'Another thing – we just got lucky! Those Indians ain't local, or they would've known about this cave. Next lot along may be. We got to get goin'!'

From her expression, she did not agree, but he solved the problem for both of them by falling asleep on his face in front of her, and by the time he wakened it was dark and impossible for either of them to track.

CHAPTER SIX

There was a steady throb which seemed to take over most of his body. His head throbbed, his hip throbbed and his thigh twitched while the stitches throbbed to a rhythm entirely their own. He felt as though he was being played by a phantom drummer with an infinite variety of drum sticks.

Cassidy knew those symptoms because he had endured them before. In Afghanistan, in India and in Mexico.

Being used to the sensations did not make them any easier to stand, either. He estimated that he had been unconscious for at least twenty-four hours which meant both that the men who had his money would be far away by now, and that the Apache had already had time to catch their quarry and have started back to follow up the signs to find

Cassidy and the woman.

They had to get moving, and they had to get moving now. He put a hand out to help himself sit up, and opened his mouth to swear when he put it almost into the hot ashes of a dying fire. Instantly a hand slapped across his mouth, and Sarah hissed angrily in his ear. He lay still and after a second, the hand relaxed and hesitantly moved away and he slept again.

He awakened the second time to the smell of cooking and the sound of water bubbling nearby. Sarah held a pine knot to the fire, and used it like a candle to stare into his face with a searching gaze.

'Fever's gone!' she said. 'Good-oh! Mama always said a good long sleep does as much good as a medicine chest, and you've had a splendid one! Feel better?'

He actually did feel a lot better. The throbbing had gone from his head and had subsided in his hip to a steady feeling of soreness. The pain had given way to an irritating itch, and he no longer felt febrile.

He did, however, feel as weak as a run-down kitten and was embarrassingly glad of the helping hand she gave him to sit up.

She poured soup into a tin cup and held him

while he drank it. He burned his mouth and swore weakly, then apologized with embarrassment.

'Don't worry! Soldier's daughter. Heard language that would skin an ox before I cut my teeth! I sometimes used to shock the RSM when I was learning to ride,' she said. Then, 'Look, do you feel up to travelling, yet? We had visitors last night, and I could have sworn they could smell the fire. They poked around the entrance for a time before they went off down the trail, and I reckon they'll be back sooner or later.'

'What kind of visitors?' He was worried more by the fact that this apparently unshakable woman was worried than by the Indians she was worried about.

'Indians, I think. Anyhow, they only went off because they heard something moving around down the trail, I think. Don't know how far they went, though.'

Not far, that was for sure. Unless they had come across a cavalry patrol. The horse soldiers were bound to be out on the plateau. It might have been that the Indians heard something more promising than following a cold trail, but it was more likely that they moved in an attempt to lure out their quarry.

'Maybe they're gone. Most like, they're still lyin''

in wait for us. We move, and they have tracks to follow. Quarry that don't move don't leave tracks,' he said.

'But if they come back?'

'They'll be back, sure as shootin'!' He paused, unwilling to alarm her further, then realized how much it would take to alarm this iron lady.

'If they get past me, save a bullet for yourself,' he said. 'Don't get took prisoner.'

'Death before dishonour? You sweet, old-fashioned thing!' she said lightly.

'Ain't dishonour I was thinkin' of, ma'am. More disembowellin' and slow fires. Don't get took, that's all, ma'am!'

The hand stirring the fire paused for a moment then resumed its stirring, this time if anything a little more vigorously.

'Message received, old thing.' She said in a more serious voice. 'Don't worry, I hadn't any intention of "getting took". American Indians aren't any more inventive than Africans, you know. Or than Afghans if it comes to that.'

She resumed feeding him, and he ate, and then rested again. Later, he awakened and found himself drinking a strange brew which tasted bitter but curiously refreshing. It made his tongue tingle, left his head strangely clear. When he asked her about it, she smiled and said: 'Green tea. Comes from China. Drink up.'

He drank, and slept again. When he woke up it was daylight outside, and the reflected light filtered up from the cavern below and threw the roof of their cave into a soft relief.

He was alone in the cave, and he swore and sat up, reaching for the gun he could see lying on a nearby rock. It was fully loaded, and he was on his knees making his way across the cave to the ladder of moke holes when he realized there was no tugging sensation in his hip, his head was clear and he felt almost back to his full strength.

He lay down at the top of the rock ladder into the lower cavern and listened intently. He could hear a rhythmic crunching somewhere deeper in the cave and recognized it once he heard a horse shift its stance and rattle its hoofs on the stone floor. It was the sound of a horse feeding contentedly.

Granted, if any passing warrior found the cave, the horses in it would tell him there was a rider somewhere nearby, but no Indian would have left the horses where they were. He would have searched the cavern and taken the ponies with him. They would represent a considerable asset to him.

He remembered the advice an old Indian fighter had told him years ago, while they sat by a camp-fire among rocks up near the Grand Canyon.

'White man'll ride a horse till he collapses, then leave him and carry on afoot. 'Tis his nature,' the big man in the battered cavalry hat had told him.

'Indian'll come along, get that horse on his feet and ride him another twenty miles till the animal dies. Then he'll eat him, smoke some of the meat and use his guts for a water carrier. Horse's gut will carry two or more gallons if you don't mind the water getting a mite gamey. To an Apache, water's water and he's drunk worse.'

The man had giggled like a girl at Cassidy's expression, but he had misunderstood it. Cassidy was remembering a long retreat down the Khyber Pass when he had carried just such a water bottle slung round his shoulders, and the taste of the water which he had sucked out of it.

Still, it had kept him alive in that long tramp through the worst country in the world, with the long barrelled jezails cracking from the rocks, and the wounded crying out on their stretchers being towed behind the surviving horses.

Still, that nasty, unnamed and unpopular little non-war was long ago and far away, and he had fought harder ones since.

'Whatever happens, we can't stay here,' he told her. 'What time is it?'

She dug into the breast pocket of her shirt and produced a watch and chain which she handed to him.

'Here, this is yours,' she said. 'I was afraid you would roll on it. Take it back.'

He glanced at the watch, which told him it was half past six. A glance out of the cave mouth told him it was morning, and that they had the day at their disposal.

He helped her gather up the remains of their kit and provisions which were pitifully small, and stow them in the saddle-bags she had also salvaged.

They had their saddles and packs and their weapons and Cassidy was not surprised to find that the weapons at least were bright, clean and shining.

CHAPTER SEVEN

Cassidy had been right and he had been wrong. The Army had tracked down the Apache and the Apache had in turn tracked down the cavalry. The result had been a pitched battle at the foot of the Rim, and both sides had left the field bloodied but unbeaten.

Cassidy and Sarah came across the Army's tracks in a narrow gully under the Rim itself and arrived to find them forted up on a little knoll among the fallen detritus of the Rim itself. The officer in command, an experienced and canny soldier named Sorensen who knew his territory and its dangerous occupants, had been progressing carefully behind a screen of scouts, and trailing a scout behind him.

The Apaches had lain in wait at the entrance to

the notch where it opened on to a shallow basin at the foot of the Rim, and the Army had failed to be surprised.

Sorensen had by a use of good tactic and crafty woodmanship himself, accordingly surprised them. The blood spots behind the rocks were too big and too bright to indicate light wounds. Though the Apache had as usual taken their casualties with them, the blood spots showed they had taken a sobering whacking, and they had retreated to lick their wounds, bury their dead and plan the whole thing over again.

Cassidy and the girl came upon the cavalry in camp, bandaging its wounded and issuing ammunition.

He pulled the horses into the side of the trail well down from the notch and scouted the position carefully before making their presence known.

'Halloo, the camp!' he called from behind a boulder large enough to be bullet proof even if the sentry were armed with a siege howitzer.

Soldiers who have recently been involved in a fight with Indians tended to be jumpy and trigger happy, and he did not want to be a casualty to his own side.

But the sentry was calm and careful. He told the

officer about the voice coming from the trail mouth behind them, and the officer told him to let them in – but carefully. Cassidy led the horses down the narrow trail between two large boulders and into the sheltered enclosure the soldiers had chosen for their campsite.

He was impressed with what he found. The bottom of the little basin was well sheltered. The horses had been picketed in a line under an overhanging rock and were feeding from their nose bags, there being little grass of any kind in the sandy depression.

Water, however, there was. A rill ran from under one of the boulders, and collected in the bottom of the depression before draining through a crack between two boulders on the downhill side, and running away out of sight. The rill was not strong, but it filled the men's canteens, then watered the horses, and now Sorensen was ready to push on at any moment.

The men were round the sides of the depression, two of them badly enough wounded to be laid out on blankets in the shade of the rocks, three neatly bandaged but mobile and watchful. Water was heating for coffee over a smokeless fire.

The officer stood up from beside one of the wounded men as Cassidy and Sarah came into his camp, and watched them come with a puzzled frown.

'Afternoon, ma'am,' he said, poking his campaign hat back on to the back of his head. 'Surprised to see a woman wanderin' around these parts at this time.'

His eyes wandered to Cassidy and noted the bloodstains on his hip and the side of his shirt. Cassidy saw the look, saw himself being recognized at least by description, and measured the distance he would have to run under the muzzles of fifteen or so guns which were accustomed to hitting moving targets. It would be suicide to run for it.

However the officer did not comment. He was after information, and the newcomers might well have it.

'Come up from Tucson, ma'am?' he asked. Cassidy shook his head.

'Down from the Rim, there,' he said. 'I met up with this lady a few nights ago, and we been lyin' up for a while.'

'You been hurt, I see,' said the officer. He would have needed a guide dog and a white stick if he had not seen the dark, hardened bloodstains on Cassidy's jeans and shirt.

'Apaches. Seems like you run into 'em, too,' said Cassidy. His was not the only blood in the sand,

and he didn't intend to let the officer imply that it was.

The man nodded, though his eyes were on Sarah, and he had the expression of a man trying to remember something. As Cassidy watched, his memory cleared.

'You'll be the English lady we've been asked to look out for, ma'am?' said the officer. 'My orders were to escort you to safety!'

Sarah looked coolly back at him. 'Depends on which English lady you have in mind, Captain,' she said, and Cassidy was strongly reminded of a colonel's lady who had once put down a minor uprising in India armed only with a ramrod back and a voice which seemed to have been forged from frozen steel.

Sorensen seemed to feel the same. Without being aware of it, he straightened his own back, and his eyes took on a wary look.

'Lady Sarah something,' he said levelly. 'Lost somewhere in the Arizona district. I've been told to look out for you and escort you back to the fort, ma'am.'

'Montague,' said Sarah. 'Lady Sarah Montague. Yes, I am she. But I am not lost. I am being guided and protected by this gentleman, here. I am in no danger, and I am certainly not going to be accompanied back to your post to be sent off somewhere at the behest of whoever is in command there.'

A slight shadow crossed the officer's face. He was not used to women like Sarah, and it showed.

'Captain Sorensen, ma'am,' he said, taking off his campaign hat to expose a thatch of yellow hair plastered down with sweat. 'Based at Fort Verde. Glad to meet ye, ma'am.'

Sarah awarded him a smile so charming a wiser man might have distrusted it on sight. But like the rest of his command, Sorensen softened like wax before a flame, and came close to wiggling. Cassidy tried hard not to snigger at the sight.

'We have been asked to look out for you, ma'am, and to offer you protection if you need it, nothin' more,' he said. 'No part of my duty to interfere with your tour.'

Sarah swung off the horse, and dropped to the ground with grace and professionalism. The eyes of every man in the little basin were fastened to her as she shook her skirt straight, and pulled her shirt tight through her belt. The effect the two simple actions had on the fit of her shirt and skirt were remarkable, but nothing to compare with the effect they had on the garrison.

There was not actually a moan of appreciation, but Cassidy felt that there should have been. He was amused though not surprised at the effect the woman had on the soldiers.

'Captain, I do appreciate your tact,' she said. 'Do you think your men could spare me a cup of that hot coffee?'

The troopers had been months, and in some cases years in the West, and few of them had so much as seen an English lady turn on the charm even before that. The effect Sarah had on them was dramatic.

Three men collided on the way to the coffee pots in the coals of the cook fires, and the cook, who took advantage of his position close to the fires, beat them all to it. A cup of steaming black coffee was on its way to Sarah before she stopped speaking.

Sarah, who had experienced hot coffee in tin cups for long enough to know how to handle it, produced a red spotted handkerchief from somewhere, and took the cup neatly and with a smile so charming Cassidy thought the cook's skin might actually have been scorched by it.

He walked over to the fire and helped himself to a cup and some coffee, and sipped it. The liquid was scalding and strong enough to float a horse shoe. After two mouthfuls he shot a glance at Sarah, whose expression of exquisite politeness would not have been out of place at a governor's garden party. She sipped her coffee with only the slightest rigidity of jaw muscles to betray her surprise at its strength.

'What is going on in the Mogollon Mesa, Captain?' she said. 'We have been dodging Indians for some time now. I thought the White Mountain Apaches were supposed to be subdued?'

Sorensen growled his men back to their posts, and hunkered down to help himself to coffee before joining Sarah and Cassidy near the fire. He was careful to keep out of direct line of sight of the gaps in the basin's rim.

'Well, ma'am,' he said, 'we were sent out to try and track a gang of bank robbers from north of here. Thought they might stir up the tribes, and it seems that's exactly what they've done. Seems there were half a dozen of them to start with, but now they're down by at least two.'

He shot a glance at Cassidy as he said it, and Cassidy met it with an expression of innocent interest. Both he and the captain knew one of the men the soldier was looking for was sitting the other side of the fire from him, sipping his coffee. Cassidy wanted to know what the captain was going to do about it, and when.

But he could not wait to find out. He put down

his cup carefully and pulled his own handkerchief from his pocket, and wiped his fingers. If the worst came to the worst he would have to take his chances. He could not involve Sarah in a gunfight, particularly one he was pretty well bound to lose.

'You can cut down your quarry some, Captain,' he said levelly. 'I found two of their bodies back down the trail. They bin killed by the Apache.

'One group got separated from the other, and they's just four left up ahead o'you. One'll be the gang leader, I reckon. Neither of the others had the money from the raid. I checked.'

'Why would you do that, friend?' Cassidy was aware of the sudden attention of the soldiers within earshot. He wanted it clear at least among the troopers that he was not a part of the bank raid gang.

'Because some of the money he has is mine. I put it in the bank just before it was raided, and I want it back. Took me a long time to earn that there cash, and I ain't goin' to let some thievin' owlhoot walk off with it.'

He stood up slowly and stretched, wincing slightly and favouring his right side where the blood had stained his jeans. If the worst came to the worst he might give himself a suggestion of an edge if the soldiers thought he was slowed down by his wound.

Sorensen pursed his lips and was about to reply when a rifle cracked outside the little depression, and a bullet howled off a rock near the horses. Startled, they plunged and tugged at their picket rope and two men ran to calm them.

The first shot was followed by a fusillade, the bullets whining viciously off the rocks, and the troopers pressed themselves into their cover and searched carefully for targets. Not a man fired in reply to the barrage of lead.

'Hold your fire until you can see the whites of their eyes!' Sorensen bellowed, and the troopers sniggered without looking round.

'Seen a stage play about the Little Big Horn,' Sorensen explained to Sarah while his own eyes examined the ground within range. 'Seems that's what Custer told his men while the Sioux was closing in on him. Felt it should be said in a real Indian battle somewhere, some time.'

He pointed his long barrelled Colt carefully and snapped a shot at the top of a tree which peered over the rim of the little fort and grunted with satisfaction when first a rifle and then a figure toppled out of it.

One of the men raised a cheer, and then they were all too busy shooting as dusty figures suddenly boiled into sight running and dropping as suddenly into cover.

Cassidy reckoned there must be at least fifteen warriors in the attacking party which meant either that the original war party had been reinforced or that a different group had taken a hand in the chase.

Either way, Sorensen and his command were in bad trouble and Cassidy and the girl were in it with him. Cassidy, annoyed with himself for allowing them to be involved, swore softly, and cocked his own revolver. It was not a long-barrelled model that Sorensen carried, and hence had not got the range. But the targets were coming obligingly closer.

He stole a glance at Sarah, and caught her looking in turn at him. She had her rifle to her shoulder and was searching the ground outside the ring of boulders methodically. She grinned at him and winked.

'Remind you of anywhere, Cassidy?' she said. 'Khyber, for instance?'

Actually, there were similarities. The dust and the hammer-hard sunshine, the brown of the rocks and the sand, and the brown bodies scurrying closer. He shot her a quick smile and simultaneously, a brown form appeared on top of a boulder just beyond her.

Cassidy shot the Apache through the throat, cutting off his scream of triumph, and kicked the body to one side as it fell forward down the face of the rock. For a moment he was tempted to fire into it again – throat wounds were not always immediately fatal – but the eyes staring upward were dead ones, and he turned away as the rim of the depression was suddenly full of Apaches, howling as they came.

For a moment he thought all was lost, as he snapped a shot at one warrior, ducked and whirled and hacked down with the barrel at a face which appeared before him. The Apache stopped in mid-stride and fell forward across his feet, bringing him down.

Another warrior was lunging at his back with a lance, and as Cassidy went down, the levelled point missed and the Apache, caught off balance, fell over the body of his fallen comrade. Cassidy caught the lance just behind its head, broke the shaft with a twist of his wrist and used the snapped-off point as a dagger.

The Apache bucked as the point drove into his chest at the join of his short ribs, and went limp.

Cassidy whipped round, to see Sarah shooting patiently at the rim of the depression, where warriors were still appearing. Her accuracy was remarkable, and he threw himself across a Winchester which had been dropped in the dust at the bottom of the depression. He spun and fired it once, twice, at the rim, found no more targets up there and swung his sights back into the mêlée.

But it was over. A few shapes were clambering back over the rim, and one threw up its arms and fell back when one of the troopers fired.

The silence which followed was mattress-heavy. The Indians were gone as though they had never been, leaving four corpses sprawled inside the perimeter in the strangely boneless heaps which said 'dead' more clearly than a surgeon. Two more had been dragged away by the retreating warriors. They would be back for the other four one way or another, for the Apaches would be determined to the point of their own death not to leave one of their number on the battlefield.

Cassidy looked for Sorensen, and found him already examining the wounded, of whom there were several. The fight had been lightning fast, savage and bloody.

Two of the troopers were dead, another two injured, one badly. Only two had escaped some form of damage in the scuffle, and Sorensen himself had a slash across his cheekbone almost exactly following the line of his old wound. It was long but not deep and like most head wounds, it was bleeding profusely.

Without a word, Sarah laid down her rifle within reach and started to help the corporal who was working on the wounded.

Cassidy walked to the line of boulders which defined the lip of the depression like battlements, and carefully surveyed the surrounding ground, first from one gap and then from another. At no time did he expose himself over the parapet.

Outside he could see nothing and had not expected to. The Apache had vanished as instantly as they had appeared, and as thoroughly.

He changed his position, careful in looking out at one side of the depression not to expose his back to fire from vantage points outside the other. The woods remained silent and apparently deserted.

'See anything?' It was Sorensen next to him on his belly, bandanna wrapped round his face and peering through the same gap. Cassidy shook his head.

'Nope. They're out there, all right. But we won't see 'em until they come again. They'll be more persistent next time. There's fewer of us, now. And they know about how many.'

'Yup.' Sorensen didn't take his eyes from the edge of the woods a little distance away, but Cassidy knew he could see no more than Cassidy.

'What are you goin' to do?' he asked the soldier. The captain for once took his eyes off the ground beyond the natural battlements, and looked at him narrowly.

'What did the posse want you for?'

Cassidy pursed his lips and scratched his unshaven neck. Sooner or later he would have to get things straight with the Army, or Arizona would be untenable for him and with or without his savings, he was determined to stay in the territory. Sooner or later it would become a state of the United States and he wanted to be there when it did.

'Money,' he said. 'Rode by Chico on my way down to some land I got in mind for horse breeding near Tucson. Stopped off for a bath and a meal at the hotel there, scrape off some of the dust and have myself a jug.'

Sorensen grinned. 'Know the feelin'!'

'Two troublemakers called McGibbon tried to shake me down, and when I objected, one of them went for his gun.'

'You kill him? Those McGibbons been asking for

it for years, now!'

'Nope. They was so slow it would'a bin murder. I made 'em shuck their guns on the floor, left their weapons on the bar and threw they out. They tried to dry-gulch me outside.'

Sorensen stared. 'And you got them first? So what's the problem? There must have been plenty o' witnesses!'

Cassidy shook his head. 'Search me. They fired and missed. I fired back and hit somebody. Didn't see who, in the dark, but there was blood in the dust when I looked. It was dark and I sure as hell didn't shoot both of 'em, so I quit lookin' and left town to make dry camp in some cottonwoods.

'Come mornin', there was a wounded man lyin' by the trail. Looked like he was tryin' to make it to the water hole, but he died while I was tendin' him. The posse came up while I was bandagin' him, and jumped to the wrong conclusion. I bin runnin' ever since!'

Sorensen gave him a long look, and pursed his lips. He wanted to believe Cassidy, but he could see the posse's problem.

'Well, seems to me the best thing for you is to turn yourself in,' he said. 'Anywhere but Chico, that is. At Chico they got a right brusque way with trials. Usually final, too!'

Cassidy stood up and stretched his arms, watching the tops of a pine beyond the perimeter. It was an obvious sniper's perch, and he had lived to his present age because he did not ignore obvious snipers' perches.

'Ma'am?' he said softly without shifting his view.

'Yes?' said Sarah tersely.

'You see that pine up there near the rim?'

'The one with the Indian in it?' Her voice was slightly muffled, and when he glanced in her direction he could see her cheek was cuddled up to the stock of her remarkable rifle. She was squinting through her telescopic sight.

'Can you get him from here?'

'No. He's behind the trunk. Can you get him to lean out?'

'I reckon. But don't you miss, now!'

'Well, don't—' the rest of her words were drowned by the flat crack of the rifle, a much quieter report from far away, and the agonized squeal of a ricocheting slug. A tiny puff of dust exploded from the rock directly in front of Cassidy's face, and he found himself flat on his stomach in the dust.

'—stick your head up,' Sarah finished. And then: 'Bloody Hell, Cass! That was a daft thing to do!'

Cassidy, spluttering dust from between his teeth wholeheartedly agreed with her, but his reaction was to relieve his feelings with an explosion of profanity. Sarah looked strongly disapproving.

'Foul language is no way to talk before a lady,' she said primly though a mouth compressed like a prune.

Cassidy, who had heard her express herself in language which would embarrass a cavalry sergeant, stared at her, nonplussed.

'Sorry, ma'am!' he said with heavy sarcasm. 'I didn't know it was your turn!'

'Well, it was!' said Sarah sourly. 'Dammit, Cassidy, I nearly killed you and that savage almost did the job for me. Keep your head down in future!'

She worked the lever of her rifle, and peered round the rock. The Indian was gone from the top of the tree, and there was a silence out there in the woods of the Rim.

'So what happened at the saloon?' said Sorensen eventually, when he came back from checking his men.

'Somebody blew the bank that night, and the posse followed one of them to the cottonwoods where I was camping. He was hit and dyin' and I was tendin' him. They jumped to the obvious conclusion!'

The soldier nodded understandingly, without taking his eyes off the perimeter.

'And now?' he said.

'I picked up Miss Sarah here havin' a spat with some Apaches in the woods, and got myself ventilated at the same time. We been holed up in a cave ever since until I come across you. That's all there is to it!'

The soldier seemed satisfied with the story, and took a look around his command. The men were tucked away into their firing positions, except for the wounded and the dying.

'Well, you better come along with us, then,' he said in the end. 'We can't stay here. We've water all right, and cover so long as there aren't too many o' the demons. But it seems to me we're fightin' more of 'em now than we were yesterday. I think they got reinforcements.'

'So?'

Sorensen looked over at his sergeant, a man called O'Rourke whom Cassidy knew and trusted, and who had been listening in to his story.

'Sounds straight enough to me, sir,' the sergeant said. 'I known Cassidy a time, and if he's a bank robber he done took it up real recent. He's a careful man with money, saves when the others are drinkin' their pay, but I never heard any man say he wasn't straight as a die! If he's been robbin' banks, he sure lucked out at it!'

Sorensen nodded his head without taking his eyes off Cassidy's face.

'You know, Cassidy, I believe you, too!' he said. 'I knew that sheriff in Chico, name of Garvin, Maurice Garvin. They call him Greasy Garvin, and if any man had it coming to him, it's Garvin. He rolled more travellers than I had hot frijoles.'

He turned to the sergeant.

'Listen up, men,' he called softly. ' We're going out of here across the Basin soon as it gets dark enough. Pack up, fill your canteens if they need it, pack your ammunition close. We'll make travoises for the wounded, and any man who can sit a horse, rides.'

He made arrangements for Cassidy and Sarah to get extra ammunition, and put Sarah in charge of the wounded.

'Hansen! Ericsson! Saddle up and get ready to ride point. We're going back down the trail towards the Fort and you are going to scout for us!'

He gave orders to bury the dead and mark their graves until the Army had time to come back and collect the corpses.

'Get ready to move. We ease out of here before full dark. Till then, keep your eyes open. They're still out there, and they're liable to make one more try before dark. Apaches don't like dying at night. Afraid their spirit won't find its way to a Happy Huntin' Ground, but I've known Apache bucks that didn't know that! Be a pity to be scalped by an ignorant one!'

CHAPTER EIGHT

Perhaps because of Sorensen's precautions, the Apache stayed back, and the detachment was able to ease out of their makeshift fort and follow its trail along the foot of the Rim towards safety unhindered.

The trail was a rough one and for the first part of the night, Cassidy led with two army scouts, picking their way along a game trail, bending low under branches and acting as a screen as well as pathfinders. It was a slow business, and the two wounded men suffered terribly as their travois legs caught on rocks and occasional tree trunks, though neither of them let out so much as a moan.

Sarah sent a message forward along the column when they came to a clearing where the first glow of the rising moon were beginning to silver the landscape and turn the shadows inky. One of the wounded men had died in the night darkness. Silent to the last he had not even given a dying moan.

Sorensen had him wrapped in his blankets and hung face down over the horse, and the travois was abandoned. The party pushed on.

Cassidy and the scouts were the first to pick up the smell of corruption at their next halt. The scout who alerted Sorensen merely grunted: 'Cassidy says bodies ahead. Wants you should come and see, sir!'

It was, Cassidy reckoned, the remains of the posse from Chico. There were only four of them, now, and only one had survived the ambush which had wiped out his mates, and by the time he had been allowed to die, he must most ardently have wished for the happy release.

Cassidy recognized him only by the remnant of his black and white cowhide vest, which had been used to blindfold him. Why, it was hard to understand, because his eyes had been put out as well. The other agonies which had been visited on him were mercifully toned down by the silver and black of the moonlight and shadows.

He was the man who had wanted to kill Cassidy without delay when the posse had found him with the dead bandit at his camp outside Chico.

'It's the posse from Chico, what's left of it,' Cassidy confirmed to Sorensen. 'This guy wanted to lynch me on the spot. The others look like they were there as well, but it ain't all of them. There's a couple more.'

'God help them if they're still alive!' said Sorensen, sombrely. 'We can't do anything for this bunch, so we'd best leave them and push on.'

They were in the process of climbing back on their horses, when one of the point scouts called in a low voice, 'Rider coming in!'

He appeared like a silver and black statue, emerging suddenly from the trees and drawing rein when he realized he was facing an Army force.

'Howdy, soldier boys!' he called, instantly putting up the back of the entire command, who loathed being addressed as 'boys', 'mind if I come in?'

'Come ahead!' Sorensen called back, and in a low voice: 'Keep your eye on him, O'Rourke! He's a man in the wrong place at the wrong time!'

But the incoming man seemed to be almost pathetically glad to see them.

'Howdy there!' he said leaning from his saddle to shake Sorensen's hand. 'Am I glad to see you blue-bellies! Thought I was all on my lonesome out with all these Injuns jest getting' ready to skin me alive!'

His eye fell on Sarah, and he took off his hat with an elaborate show of civility.

'Pardon me, ma'am,' he said. 'Didn't forget my manners, jest plain didn't see you there!'

Sorensen was impatient to get going, but he needed any local information he could get. 'What happened to you, then, Mr . . . er. . . ?'

The newcomer rammed his hat back on his head, and leaned forward over his saddle horn. 'Grosser. Pete Grosser, Captain,' he said. 'Set out with a posse from up to Chico, chasing a bunch of murderin' bank robbers, got separated from the rest of the guys last night. I was out scoutin' when the injuns hit 'em! I heard what was happenin' but I got no chance to help. Terrible things, terrible things I heard. . . .'

He seemed to be unstoppable, but Sorensen had a command full of nervous trigger-happy men and a woman he had to get to safety somehow, and little time.

'Fall in behind the lady,' he said sharply. Sarah's place in the middle of the column put Grosser firmly into custody. He had half the command behind him and half in front, and with Indians all around them, there was nowhere for the man to run.

*

The dawn came in like a cavalry charge, first the duck-egg blue of first light, then the glowing gold of full daybreak, and the hint of the heat of the day to come. There were some dark, mounded clouds on the horizon, but they seemed too small and far away to matter. Sorensen called a halt for the men and horses to take a drink of water and the troopers pack away their warm coats from the night time journey.

Cassidy, who was uneasy about Grosser, rode back down the column to check on Sarah, and was aware of a sudden shadow in the glory of the morning as he pulled his horse up near to her.

Grosser was watering his horse from his hat and glanced up as Cassidy reined in. His reaction was rattlesnake fast and totally unexpected. He swore, grabbed for his gun and so startled his horse that it reared, put one hoof off the edge of the trail and fell sideways down the slight slope on the downhill side.

At the same moment, Grosser's gun went off, Cassidy, caught half in and half out of the saddle, saved himself from his own horse's startled plunge only by grabbing the saddle horn.

And the world turned to water.

For just a second, Cassidy was so taken up with hanging on to the plunging animal that he thought he had fallen somehow into some water. Then, still hanging on to the horse's reins for grim death, he realized one of the monsoon rain storms characteristic of the country had struck. It was, for a moment, like trying to breathe inside a waterfall.

Dimly through the rain, he could occasionally catch a glimpse of a trooper fighting like Cassidy to keep his mount under control. The horses were whinnying desperately, the soldiers were swearing, and Cassidy heard, shockingly, first one and then another report.

He managed to get his leg over the saddle and brought his horse under control, just as it shimmied sideways into another horse, and stopped bucking.

As fast as it had started, the rainstorm slackened and began to run out. It had lasted less than a quarter of an hour, yet the ground was running with water as though the trail led straight through a lake. Cassidy quieted the horse, shook his soaked hat to get off the excess water, and looked around for Grosser. He could see the man's horse down the slope like a reef against the flood water running past it.

It was making weak attempts to stand up, though one foreleg was broken and the bone sticking through the hide. There was no sign of its rider, and when he looked around, none of Sarah, either. Her charge, the second wounded man, was lying on his travois half on and half off the trail, and his horse was missing.

The wounded soldier was dead, shot through the head at such close range that there were powder burns around the wound.

Cassidy scrambled down the slope to the crippled horse, took a careful aim and shot it through the head. He could see without searching that the saddle-bags which had weighed so heavily on the horse's flank were missing, along with its rider.

Sorensen came back along the trail, examined the soldier's corpse, and slid down the slope to join Cassidy. He was plainly beside himself, and his jaw muscles were corded with the effort of keeping his temper.

It was several seconds before he got himself under control enough to speak.

'He was a good man,' he said. 'Had a wife and child back at Verde, just about done his time and he was talking about signing on for another stretch. He'd have been a sergeant if he had.'

He took off his hat and wiped the band with his bandanna, then rammed it back on savagely.

'Where is the bastard?' he said, savagely. 'Took a shot at me as the rain hit, or at any rate, I thought he did. May have been shooting your trooper instead.'

'What in the name of all that's holy, did he want to do that, for?'

'Needed his horse, I guess! His own was crippled. He had some pretty heavy saddle-bags to transport, and I guess they had the money from the bank in 'em. Maybe other loot, too.'

'You don't believe he was in the posse, then?'

'Do you? Apaches may be a lot o' things, but they ain't careless! If he was with the posse, how come the Apache didn't see him?'

'No, I reckon he was one of the raiders held up the bank. He wasn't with the posse, he was doin' his damnedest not to be. The Indians must have been like the cavalry riding to his rescue. All he had to do was lie low, and wait for the Apache to finish their business and go on their way.'

'And then?'

'And then we come along, the real cavalry ridin' to his rescue – with the one snag that I was with you. I saw the whole of the posse, and sure as shootin' he wasn't with it, that I'll swear!'

He turned to his horse, settled the cinch which had slipped during his fight with the animal, and swung into the saddle.

'Where you going?' said Sorensen stupidly, and

swore at himself.

'Why, to get that lady back and have a look in them heavy saddle-bags. If what I believe is true, Grosser or whatever his real name it, was one of the raiders, and since he's finished up with the loot, I reckon he was probably the leader.'

Sorensen looked harassed. It was his duty to report to the general at the first, but at the same time there was an English noblewoman in his area who had been kidnapped, and who was now his responsibility.

Cassidy watched all this parade across his face, and grinned.

'Sorry, Cap! I ain't got time to waste. That young woman's my responsibility!'

He turned the horse, and rode off down the only path the fleeing Grosser could possibly have taken, downhill and into the trees.

CHAPTER NINE

Cassidy found the first button where the fine line of the game trail separated to go round a rocky outcrop. It was hanging on a branch at eye height, but it was so tiny that if it had not been attached to a scrap of material, he could easily have missed it.

It was one of the buttons off Sarah's shirt, and as he followed along the path it indicated, he kept his eyes peeled. Some time later he was wondering if he had missed one along the way when he came across another. This was at the point where the trail deviated towards the cliff, and a secondary track, very faint, swung down into the basin.

Reassured that he had not missed one on the way, he swung down the track and found tracks in the rapidly drying mud along the path. The heat of the day was soaking up the fallen rain and making the air soggy and sweaty. It would dry out soon, he knew, but at the moment, it was making mud where he needed mud, and he could read the hoof prints, now.

The horse carrying heaviest was in front, for the hoof prints of the lighter horse overlaid them in places. Grosser was a big man, and the cavalry horse he was riding had military plates, as did Sarah's borrowed mount. It was definitely them.

He realized, then, where they were aiming for. There was a shallow cave in the cliff foot under a tumbled rock slab. It was a recess rather than a true cave, and there was only one way in and out, so it had its limits as a hideout, but it was defensible.

It was also known to the local Apache, and Cassidy knew it as a death-trap rather than a hideout. He urged the horse on faster, now that he did not need to look for tracks, and closed on the hideout.

Grosser was, predictably, having trouble with Sarah. To the outlaw she must have looked like a tasty bonus when he murdered the wounded cavalryman to steal his horse, and in any case he could not leave her behind him as a witness and a guide to the direction he had taken.

Instead, she was turning out to be a nightmare.

Awkward, prickly and haughty, she constantly sneered at him and refused to do as she was told. Eventually his temper snapped. He back-handed her hard and when she spat curses at him for it, he resolved to finish with her, quickly. The shallow cave hideout was close at hand, and would be a good place to carry out his plans, and a convenient place to leave the body.

He steered the horses under the vast rock slab and tethered them at the back of the cave, and carefully put the girl's odd rifle and his own Winchester on his own saddle.

'Build a fire!' he snarled at her, and when she spat a refusal, he grabbed for her, determined to teach her a lesson.

The knife came as a complete surprise. One moment, she was sneering at him through swollen lips, eyes filled with hate – the next, his face was bleeding down his shirt and his cheek was laid open almost to the bone.

He just managed to duck away from a second rattlesnake-fast strike with the glittering blade, and she was stalking him in the confined cave, half crouched like a practised knife fighter, empty hand wound in a bundle of her shirt and held in front of her as a shield, her right hand drawn back. He could see the light reflected from the blade, which must be sharp enough to shave with.

His jaw line was on fire, and his shirt sticking to his chest with blood, running from his cheek. He was both consumed with a murderous rage and for the first time in his life afraid of a woman. He had thought to capture an easy victim and instead found himself trapped in an enclosed space with a she-wolf.

There was nothing else for it: he would have to kill her without taking any further risks. Raging with frustration and shame, he reached for his gun.

'Move another inch,' said Cassidy's voice behind him, pleasantly, 'and I'll break your back and leave you for the Apaches!'

'Bugger the Apaches,' Sarah said in a rattlesnake hiss. 'Hold him while I deal with him! He'll beg for the Apaches before I let him die!'

Cassidy stepped into the cave, his Colt in hand. He was a frightening figure, his jeans in tatters, his shirt hanging in strips from his shoulders. His hat was drying out, but its soaking in the downpour had left it in a woeful shape.

His pistol, however, was clean and dry and Grosser could see down the barrel. He saw his own death, there, and he was paralysed.

'Take the gun from his belt,' Cassidy told Sarah,

'without getting between me and him. Don't kill him yet. I need to know something, and he is going to tell me!'

Grosser looked into his eyes and knew he was speaking the truth. One way or another, he knew he would talk, no matter what this man asked. He also knew that in the end, he would die.

He moved back against the wall of the cave, and as he did so, knocked his leg hard against its uneven surface. It hurt and he winced and reached down his hand in an automatic reflex to rub it.

When his straightened up again, the knife which he carried in his boot was already in his hand, and he turned the motion of straightening into a lightning fast throw.

Cassidy saw the knife as it emerged from Grosser's boot, and shouted a warning to Sarah as he hurled himself sideways. The thrown knife missed him by a thickness of his shirt, but Sarah's knife did not miss.

The black knife she kept in her waistband was indeed sharp enough to shave with; her soldier father had sworn it was better steel than they made in Sheffield. The short, spear-point blade went between Grosser's ribs with hardly a catch, and blood bubbled into his throat even as it poured through his shirt.

He went down like a shot deer, the strength going out of his legs as the air bubbled through his ribs.

Sarah, her hand covered in his blood, stepped back as he fell and held her knife ready for any trickery, but there was no time left for trickery.

Grosser peered at Cassidy as the man leaned over him.

'So she got me in the end,' he rasped. 'Should'a known. My ma always said women would be the end of me! She weren't often wrong, my ma! She had the sight!'

'Pity you didn't!' Sarah said to him matter of factly.

'Maybe not, but I can tell you your future!' the dying man rasped. His eyes were clouding, but the urge to hurt still ran strong in him.

'You think you're goin' to get out o' this basin alive? Not a chance!'

'Why not?' Cassidy didn't really care. But he did want to know what Grosser thought.

'You're in on the start of the biggest Indian war this territory ever saw!' the dying man coughed, and blood sprayed. He clamped his hand over the gap between his ribs to give himself breath to deliver his venom.

'We bin killin' Indians for weeks. All Indians! Apaches wherever they were, anything with dark skin and black hair! Nothin' they hate more than a scalp hunter, and we bin scalpin' every Indian we laid hands on!'

He coughed. Blood sprayed. 'Jicarillas, Tontos, White Mountain, Chirichuas, you name 'em! Crook wants peace and law in the Territory? No way! Ever' Indian between here and. . . .'

Where exactly they were never to learn. His breath bubbled for one last time, and the hating eyes lost their focus and started to glaze over.

CHAPTER TEN

The faint light of the early morning reached a probing finger through the trees and surroundings turned from stark black into half-tones of colour. There was a light mist hanging around the tree trunks which would burn off within a few minutes, but at this fragile moment in time, laid an eerie unreality upon the forest.

Cassidy could hear a faint ripple of sound away towards the cliff face, which told him they were near one of the tiny run-offs from the rim above them. The music of the falling water made the morning delightful, and the scout wondered for a wistful moment if this land would ever be a safe place to enjoy such moments.

He checked the slowly emerging undergrowth with his eyes and ears as the light strengthened before eventually rising from the pile of rocks in which they had made their brief camp in the pre-dawn hours, and checked the horses.

He had unsaddled the beasts when they stopped last night, and had been sitting with his back propped against the saddle-bags which were half under a large rock. A wry grin tugged at his lips as he reflected that when he was flat broke he had slept lightly but well because all he had to lose was his life.

Now, he slept lightly but badly because he also had his hard earned stash and the girl to worry about. He was surprised to find them a greater burden than his life had been.

The thought made him lean down and check the sleeping girl. She had wriggled herself down on the underside of a sloping rock, and he frowned because in the dark there had been no way of telling if there had been a previous and possibly venomous occupant of the space. However, all seemed well and he laid a finger gently behind her ear until the touch roused her from her sleep.

She opened her eyes silently and was instantly awake. Her first action, he saw with approval, was to check on her rifle beside her in the blankets, and check the loads in the revolver she had salvaged when Grosser dropped it in the canyon trap.

Satisfied about her arms, she took a small swig from her canteen and washed her mouth out before swallowing a mouthful.

While she was doing all that, she surveyed the surroundings carefully and methodically. Cassidy who already knew there was no unseen watcher, watched her instead with approval and pleasure, and wished he had time to do more.

'What now?' Sarah asked him as they stopped by the tiny rill in the rocks for a wash and to replenish their canteens. Grosser had stocked himself up with a surprisingly good pack of food. There was rice and bacon, flour and coffee and some beans. There were bullets, too, in the saddle-bags, and a razor and soap wrapped in a scrap of towel.

'We get out o' here and back to civilization where I can get rid o' this cash and get the law off my back,' said Cassidy, wrapping a hunk of campfire bread round some cooked bacon and handing it over to her. The girl looked at it, and then bit into it with a look of pleasurable surprise. She washed it down with a swig from the tin mug of coffee they were sharing.

'I say, you learned to cook somewhere or other!'

she said. 'This is the best camp-fire bread I ever tasted!'

He nodded and pointed at the saddle-bags at his feet. 'Grosser looked after hisself better than the other owlhoots,' he said. 'His supplies are pretty good. About time we got something back from the thievin' bast— er, the crooked sidewinder!'

She shot an amused look at him and grinned like an urchin.

'What now? There must be some sort of reward for the bank raiders,' she pointed out. 'Bring them in and the law will be inclined to take you more seriously.'

Cassidy kicked dirt over the fire until he had quenched the flames, and doused the ashes with the coffee grounds. The idea had occurred to him, but there was the girl to be considered.

'I'd prefer to get you to safety and get the money to General Crook. He'll know what to do with it. I know him!'

'And more important, he knows you,' she finished. 'As I am beginning to. All right, Cassidy, let's go, then!'

The horses had slaked their thirst at the little basin under the falling water. From the water mark on it, the level was already falling since the rain had let up, and by morning, there would be only a trickle coming down the cliff. In two days, a man would have to dig for what was left.

They rode all morning following the foot of the cliff face, and staying out of sight among the trees until they petered out. Ahead of them was a steadily narrowing canyon, in the brown of the grass and rocks.

It also made a good fort, there in the mouth of the canyon, and he had a feeling they were being followed. It was so familiar to him that he did not even question it.

Whoever was back there in the land behind them was keeping his distance, and Cassidy wanted him where he could be identified and if necessary eliminated. By which he meant 'shot'.

Behind him along the trail there was a tidy sum in repeating rifles which he could not carry, and which he would much prefer the Indians not to have, but that would soon become the Army's problem, and he was only too glad to leave it to them.

The cabin ruins were tucked back against the side of the pass, just where it narrowed. Beyond, he could see the mountains where the land became a maze of gullies and passes. At this time of year they were brown.

They camped within the low walls which had once been the foundations of the cabin.

Sarah helped unsaddle the horses and wiped down their backs. The one she was riding looked as though it might be developing a saddle gall, and she treated it with special care. The horse shifted its hips uneasily but submitted to her handling.

Cassidy watched her silently while he saw to his own mount. She was, he admitted, a good horsewoman in every way. She rode like a cowhand, understood her mount, and genuinely cared about the animal's comfort and good health. He was thinking about it while he made a fire and cooked some bacon and biscuits in the bacon fat. By the time Sarah had finished handling the horses he had their meal ready and they ate standing while he resaddled the horses.

The horses themselves were a sure signal that something was wrong. Cassidy's kept looking back up the trail with his ears pricked, and stamped restlessly.

'Is there someone behind us?' asked Sarah as she pulled the cinches tight on her own pony, then punched it expertly in the gut and pulled the cinch up another notch while it winced.

'Sneaky old thing! Next time I won't even bother wiping your back!' she told it. The horse rolled its eyes at her, but made no attempt to nip her, which she said was a bonus.

'How far are we from the fort?' she asked.

'Rest of today and all tomorrow, barring Injuns, owlhoots and posses,' Cassidy told her with the long, level look she was beginning to recognize as his version of a sly grin.

The pass was narrowing as they went along, and Cassidy's nerves tightened accordingly. In the wide mouth of the canyon, there was room for manoeuvre. Here in the gut, it was more restricted and without the asset of tight, concealing curves he might have got in a slot canyon. He was restricted, but the restriction gave him less concealment, not more.

Sarah was riding with her rifle in hand, butt resting on her thigh and barrel pointing at the sky. Her head swung from side to side like the turret on one of the new naval monitors, restlessly seeking a target.

They were in the narrowest part of the canyon when he heard a stone click in the oppressive, still heat. Both horses stopped as if on a signal, and Sarah's strained its head to look back.

There was a natural bay in the canyon wall a little ahead, and he gestured her into it, gave her the lead rein for his horse, slipped out of the saddle and carefully retraced his steps along the wall.

He had not gone far before another stone rattled and then a third. He was too close to the canyon wall to see what was making the noise, and did not want to expose his position by stepping out, so he hunkered down by a rock and waited.

A stone clicked again, and he heard a muffled exclamation, and pulled the rifle tight into his shoulder while picking the exact spot on the canyon floor at which he would fire.

When the follower did eventually show himself, however, Cassidy eased his finger off the trigger with enormous care, and let his shoulders relax.

The follower was Sergeant O'Rourke, and he was leading his mount by the reins. As Cassidy watched, the horse kicked another stone, and Cassidy grinned at the exasperation on the soldier's face. O'Rourke looked like a recruit's bad dream at the best of times, but the frustration of towing behind him a noisy nuisance he could not do without had deepened every line until his eyes were well nigh buried.

Cassidy was about to call out when a shadow on the canyon wall behind the soldier moved slightly, and turned into an Apache stealthily emerging from cover to aim at O'Rourke's back.

There was not time to shout a warning and Cassidy simply shifted his aim a couple of inches and fired. The bullet kicked a fountain of dust from the canyon wall, and the Apache vanished simultaneously. Whether he had been hit or not, Cassidy could not tell, but O'Rourke was not waiting to find out.

As the shot sounded, he spun and in one motion threw his leg over the saddle. The horse, trained to fast reactions, went off like a race champion with the old soldier hanging on to the reins and the saddle horn, and slamming in his heels to get more speed.

At the same time, there were a barrage of shots, and a series of puffs of dust followed him along the canyon floor, until he vanished round the bend.

The next shot flicked splinters of stone past Cassidy's face, and he hit the ground running. Once again, the canyon was resounding with gunshots, until he reached the bend and ran out of range.

He slid round the corner of the girl's refuge and found himself looking down the barrel of her rifle.

'This,' he growled, swatting it aside, 'is getting to be too much of a habit, ma'am! Point it at the bad guys, why don't you?'

'Well, you smell pretty rancid yourself!' Sarah

snapped. 'Try yelling before you come round the corner, Cassidy! I haven't got ammo to waste!'

The Apaches having lost their element of surprise, had abandoned concealment and were yelling like demons. There was firing from round the bend, which suggested that the main body of the Army force was coming under attack, and a moment later, he heard O'Rourke's voice calling from further down the pass.

'Cassidy! You there, dammit? Cash Cassidy!'

'Sure I'm here,' the scout returned, in an irritated voice. 'Where else would I be? Are there Army patrols, Apaches and owlhoots shootin' someplace else? Did I miss somethin'?'

'Yeah, lawmen!' the sergeant called. 'We got two o' them back with the column. If they survived, that is!'

Bad language seemed inadequate for the way Cassidy felt at the moment. His clothing was in tatters, he had a hole in his hide, his money had been stolen and he had been accused to stealing it, of murder, and the Lord knew what else.

Now, it seemed the law had joined the Army and the Apache in the pursuit of Cashel Cassidy and his hard earned cash. And all because he had fancied a hot meal he had not cooked himself, a jug of strong drink and a night in a bed.

He was mad clear through, and a Cassidy with a gun on his hand and blood in his eye was a man to be avoided by anything less than a regiment with artillery support and a squadron of cavalry, preferably heavy.

A slug spanged off the rock above his head, and by chance he happened to be looking in the right direction and saw the warrior raise his rifle for another shot.

Cassidy nailed him with a snap shot from the Winchester, and worked the lever swiftly enough to have a round in the chamber just as another tried to change position. He hit that one, too, though from the howl of rage and pain, not fatally.

The firing from round the bend was diminishing, and he ran a little way out into the pass, and saw a blue-clad cavalryman running down the far wall, firing as he came. Bullets raised puffs of dust along the wall near one man, and he stopped and raised his Springfield to his shoulder aiming back across the pass at Cassidy's side. The heavy carbine thumped into the man's shoulder, and a rifle clattered down the face of a large boulder just over Cassidy's head and fell on to the floor of the pass.

Other troopers were advancing down the pass, firing as they came, and suddenly the rocks were dotted with fleeing dust-coloured figures. The failed ambush was over and the Apache were making their escape.

Sarah emerged carefully from the little gully which had been her refuge, leading the horses with reins wrapped over her arm, and with her rifle carried at the high port. She sighed with relief and aggravation when she saw Cassidy.

'I saw you run out of my sight, and I thought they had got you,' she said testily. 'I really wish you would take more care, Cassidy! It's the Army's job to kill Indians, not yours!'

'You'd better believe it! If we'd been Indians, I'd 'a shot you by now!' Sorensen told him from behind, with deep sincerity.

'And you better remember Apaches ain't the only ones can get mad!' Cassidy snapped. 'Me, I'm mad enough to tie! Where the hell you bin since that damn rain squall? I bin near drowned, near shot, near scalped, and near stripped jay-bird naked. My pants is in shreds, my shirt's tore up, I got holes in me and I killed more Apaches than the Seventh Cavalry.'

'Well—' Sorensen began.

'Well, hell! First thing you kin do is take charge of these bank takin's, less my bankroll. I worked damn hard for that money, fought Mexican bandits, Indians, bank robbers and just the cursed weather! I baked, fried, froze and damn near drowned – and all for some sneakin' bank robber to take it off me?

'I don't think so! I really, truly do not think so!'

Sorensen took advantage of his sheer lack of breath to interrupt.

'There's two deputies from the US marshal's office in Tucson here. They're asking for you!'

He winced at the ferocity in the surprisingly clear blue eye the scout turned on him.

'Bring 'em on!' said. 'Two US marshals is all I need today!'

CHAPTER ELEVEN

The two men who came from the rear of the battered column were no advertisement for the rule of law and order, to be sure, thought Cassidy. They were an ill-matched pair, too.

One was a tall, bony man in a dark check shirt and jeans, his boots downtrodden and his leather vest scuffed and rubbed with use. His badge was hooked into one of the bullet loops on his gunbelt, and surprisingly shiny and new, considering the shabbiness of the rest of the man's gear.

He had a prominent Adam's apple which bobbed spasmodically and he was chewing tobacco which had left a stain down the side of his mouth under his straggly moustache.

The other was a powerful, ginger haired man with eyelashes so pale they were almost invisible, and a freckled, pale skin which had burned red in the sun. He had on a buckskin shirt, jeans and a low crowned black hat with a flat brim which he kept tilted forward over his eyes. His badge, too, was very shiny and new.

'This is Milt Tranter, and his partner there is Ed Curry, out of Tucson,' said Sorensen in a noticeably neutral voice.

'Howdy, ma'am,' said Tranter, without taking his eyes off Cassidy and the saddle-bags he was carrying. Curry merely nodded. He, too, was watching Cassidy.

Sarah did not reply, but busied herself with her horse's harness, settling the saddle firmly and tightening the cinch unnecessarily. When she tuned back to the group, she had her rifle in her arms. Cassidy wondered if he was the only one who had heard her cock it.

The saddle-bags, which were hanging over his shoulder, masked the Colt he had pushed into his waistband behind his belt buckle. The other gun – his own – was in plain sight in his holster. Both men were watching it, and neither of them had the thong over the hammer of their own guns. If the showdown was now, he had better shoot fast and straight.

'We bin sent up from Tucson to find a man held up the bank in Chico,' said Tranter. 'Information is that he's headin' down this way, and we come to head him off!'

'From Tucson,' said Cassidy, thoughtfully. 'Fair step, Tucson. You must 'a made good time, on horseback.'

The alternative was walking, and it would have taken them weeks on foot, over the desert landscape, crossing Indian territory and without water. He had as good as called them liars, which was exactly what he thought of them.

Tranter's fair skin reddened even under his sunburn as he took in the implication, and he opened his mouth to give a hot reply, which was cut off sharply by his lanky partner.

'Never mind where we bin – who're you and where you bin in the last couple of days?' he asked. His hand was hanging very close to his gun, and Cassidy eased the pistol out from behind his belt buckle under cover of the saddle-bag, and eased back the hammer with his left thumb.

'Perhaps I can be of some help here. For the past week, Mr Cassidy has been guiding and guarding me through the Tonto Basin,' said Sarah.

She smiled with such limpid sweetness that Cassidy got ready to duck. Sarah in sweet and reasonable mood was a woman poised to strike.

The unexpected interruption threw Curry off

balance, and Tranter switched his eyes from the loaded saddle-bag to the handsome woman.

His eyes became wary, and he eased backwards a pace. Sarah turned towards Curry and the rifle followed her eyes. Curry's face took on the same wary look as his companion.

'What Mr Cassidy says is quite correct,' she said, her smile warm enough to melt wax. 'You have made remarkable time from Tucson. I had allowed a week to get there from here, and that was moving fast on good horses.'

Cassidy had not taken his eyes off Tranter who he had identified as the really dangerous one of the pair because he was a hair quicker on the uptake than his colleague.

'Maybe best not to confuse these *hombres*, ma'am,' he said gently. 'They can't have bin deputies for long. Likely to be a mite jumpy in formal situations like this here. Am I right, boys?'

Curry's eyes switched back to him. He looked tense and uncertain of himself. He had been expecting a straight switch for Cassidy from Army custody to his own, and an immediate get-away. He had not been aware of Sarah's involvement in the equation, and he did not know exactly how to take her.

She sounded English and prissy, but she

handled the rifle like a soldier. The troopers clearly knew Cassidy very well and that was also a factor he had not expected. He had not prepared any arguments to the contrary.

'We bin deputies for years,' protested Tranter. 'What makes you think we're new to the job?'

'For years? Oh, that explains it,' said Sarah. 'We were just remarking on how very new and clean your badges of office seem to be! Now I understand. The originals must have worn out, and these are the new replacements!'

It sounded so ridiculous that a few of the listening troopers sniggered. Sorensen's face was a study in self control.

It was, unexpectedly, Tranter who saved the situation and incidentally his own life. He stepped forward, right hand extended in a placatory gesture and well away from his gun.

'Now, let's all calm down a mite and step back, here,' he said. 'The lady seems to be unhappy about the time it took us to get here. The answer is that we wasn't in Tucson, we was in Phoenix. Meeting you here was just dumb luck!'

'Luck?' said Sorensen cynically. ' I thought you were looking for us?'

'Yeah, but we found you first crack out o' the box! Then Cassidy and the lady here turn up as well, and I began to think we done somethin' right! Both lots of people we was lookin' for all at the one time!'

Sorensen's face told its own story. He did not believe a word of it, but he had no proof one way or the other. One thing was sure, the English noblewoman was not leaving his sight again until he could hand her safely over to the general at the Fort.

Cassidy he was not able to do anything about. He was certain the scout was telling the truth, but the man had admitted having the bank loot hanging over his shoulder at this very moment, and it was Sorensen's clear duty to take possession of it and return it to the legal owners. Under some circumstances, he might have been inclined to let Cassidy take the portion of the loot he claimed belonged to him.

But now, all that was changed. The two lawmen – and he had no proof they were anything else – said they had warrants for Cassidy and the money, and Phoenix was certainly a secure place to take both.

On the other hand, from what he had seen of Sarah, she was not a woman to be given orders, even if he thought she was likely to take the slightest notice of them.

Certainly it would be his head on the block if he allowed two men of whom he had deep suspicions to take both Cassidy and the money off with them into the desert, never mind whatever might happen to Lady Sarah.

They would all have to go back to the Fort with his detail, and General Crook would be able to sort things out there.

Having come to this conclusion, he also came to another.

'Right, you two have a warrant for Cassidy, here? Let's see it,' he asked abruptly, and noted the flicker of expression which crossed both faces simultaneously.

'Warrant's with our Tucson office,' said Curry quickly, 'You can see it down there, if you want.'

Sorensen shook his head. 'No, I can't get down to Tucson, even if Chico was in the Tucson jurisdiction, which it isn't,' he said unnecessarily. In the current conditions, General Crook with a battery of mountain guns could not guarantee Sarah's safety on such a journey, and the invitation was ridiculous. On the other hand, he was committed to returning her to the safety of an Army post, and Fort Verde had a perfectly good telegraph from which to contact the Fort at Tucson.

'You want Cassidy, you'll have to come along

with me to the Fort,' he said. 'You can depend on my protection to get you there, but after that, of course, you'll be on your own!'

He pulled on his gloves and swung into his saddle, making a circle in the air with his right hand.

'Mount up!' roared O'Rourke, climbing aboard his own mount, and the two self-proclaimed lawmen were forced to follow their example or lose their prisoner and his carefully guarded saddle-bags.

Formed up into a loose column, the command, with Cassidy and Sarah riding behind Sorensen, resumed the way down the pass towards the trail to Fort Verde. Curry and Tranter tailed on behind, pulling their bandannas over their mouth and nose against the dust. Sorensen might be forced to take them along with him but he knew of nothing which forced him to keep them out of the dust.

'I don't like the look of those two,' Sarah told Cassidy in ringing tones which must be clearly heard by Sorensen. 'Those badges are entirely too shiny and new for one thing. And if they were in Phoenix, how did they get up here so quickly? We have only been making our way west for a couple of days.'

Cassidy, who had assessed them as fakes as soon

as he laid eyes on them, tipped his hat over his eyes and glanced sideways at her.

'You're right not to trust 'em,' he said. 'The thin one's called Cord Sangster and the red head's Billy Bascombe. Both wanted men, both killers. Question is, where they bin and how did they know we'd got the bank loot back?'

Sarah nodded. 'Not in Phoenix, I'll trow!'

'Trow?'

'I'll bet, then. Warrant, swear, believe, guess! How many words d'you want, dammit!'

'Jes' the ones I c'n unnerstand, ma'am, jes' the ones I c'n unnerstand,' he said laconically and spurred his horse up to ride with Sorensen.

'What do you think on those two, Captain? Know 'em from anyplace?'

'No, but I reckon I should,' admitted the officer, putting a hand on his horse's back as he turned to look down the column. It was raising its own plume of dust, now, and he was uncomfortably aware that searching eyes could hardly miss it.

Cassidy told him the names of the two men and his own suspicions, and Sorensen nodded soberly as he listened.

'Trouble is, half the lawmen in the territory have been on the wrong side of the law one time or another. Even the Earps got a few questions hanging over their heads.

'You hear about that gunfight down to Tombstone with the hard bunch they used to call The Cowboys?'

There was hardly a man in Arizona who had not, and Cassidy had to admit it. But Tranter and Curry did not come anywhere near the reputation of the Earps who had been on the side of the law at any rate by reputation for years.

'Tell you somethin' else is botherin' me,' Cassidy said. 'Where did all this Indian trouble start this time? I ain't heard of any big fights with the Tonto Apaches for a while, and yet this here area's alive with war parties. Ain't just a few bucks on the prod for trouble and a reputation. The Injuns is thicker'n fleas on a dog's back, and they are rarin' for a fight!'

Sorensen had to agree with this. He, too, had been wondering what had put a fire under the tails of all the Indians in the Tonto basin at once.

'I seen half a dozen different lots of tracks, all from different parties,' he admitted. 'There's somethin rilin' them up!'

'And when did you last hear of Apaches takin' on an Army group as big as this one, just for the hell of it? Time to time they'll hit an Army patrol when a few bucks want to get their bloodin', but

Injuns ain't no more daft than white men. They don't pick fights they can only lose. 'Cept when they're real mad about somethin' and on the prod.'

'You're working your way round to something. Spit it out!' the officer said, testily. He was watching a slight haze of dust ahead and off to the right, just where he would have to swing north to follow the trail which climbed along the side of Deadman's Mesa, and he would have to swing that way soon.

'You see that dust up ahead?' he asked.

'Bin watchin' it a while,' said Cassidy laconically. He had seen it some time back.

'What d'you reckon?'

'Them Indians sure are mad,' opined the scout. 'I'd say that there's another ambush. They got no joy with the last, so there must be somethin' different about this one. But they ain't stupid. They must know that anybody who ain't actually asleep can see that there dust. They're tryin' to push you to go some other trail, where there ain't no dust and they got somethin' waitin' for you a'ready!'

Sorensen got out his field glasses and raked the hillside ahead of them. There was no sign of Indians, but then, there would not be. What he was looking for was something – anything – out of place. And he found it.

'There's a patch of scrub down along the trail there on the east side of the mesa,' he said, handing the field glasses to Cassidy. 'See anything there?'

'Somethin' glittering,' Cassidy confirmed. ' and a mite further along, there's another. You wouldn't see it from closer up. I reckon they're tryin' to push you away from the top trail and on to that one. Only thing – that there's a dead end. That's how the mesa got its name.'

'We'll keep to the higher path and go round the west side of the mesa,' confirmed the officer, and tucked his field-glasses back into the case. 'Sergeant! Swing west over the shoulder of the mesa there!'

'Yo!' replied O'Rourke, turning in his saddle to issue the orders, and the column turned over the shoulder of the ridge and started up the west side of the mesa.

Cassidy dropped into line next to the officer, who gave him a long, hard look under the brim of his hat.

'What the hell is happening round here, Cassidy?' he said in a voice which had a warning in it.

'Me, I think we're headin' for a fair to middlin'

Indian uprisin',' Cassidy told him simply. 'And it ain't just local, Cap! I been runnin' into Apaches for the last few days!'

'No kidding?' said Sorensen. 'I thought they were the Episcopalian Church on a recruitment drive!'

Cassidy obliged him with a grin.

'Ladies' choir an' all?' he said. 'No, it's better than that. Local Apaches are the Tonto Apaches, right?'

'Nice to have an expert along, particularly since we're in the Tonto Basin,' growled the officer. 'Get on with it!'

Cassidy leaned back and pulled the broken arrow from his blanket roll. He smoothed the feathers and held it out.

'You ever seen a Tonto arrow like that one?'

Sorensen had served in the area for years, and knew about the Apache arrow marks. He took the arrow in a gloved fist and examined it.

'No,' he admitted. 'Tontos are in the woods. They can get wood for their shafts. This one's reed stem and wood. Looks more like. . . .' He hesitated.

'Looks more like Chiricahua work,' Cassidy finished for him, 'They ain't got that much straight wood stems to choose from over in the desert, so they use what they can get. Strong reed stems, with solid wood front and back end. Straight as they come and fly true, and when they hit, they go right in and often break off. They're the very devil to get out, and while they are in, they're doin' damage.'

'I know,' said Sorensen. 'We had a kid over at Fort Apache who got one in the lung. He made it back to the fort, all right, but died a couple of days later. When the MO cut him open, his lung was totally solid. Full of stuff. Couldn't breathe!'

'Yeah, well the Northern Chiricahuas are stuck in the desert. Don't get many straight shafts from the trees, and they make them out of cactus stems and when they can find them, reeds. This here's one of 'em. Now what's a desert Chiricahua doin' up here in Tonto land?'

'There's Apaches aplenty on the San Carlos. All kinds, too. None of them like it, and I don't blame 'em.'

'But what are they doin' up here, in the Tonto, right now? All of 'em? What you got here, Captain, ain't a few raiders, it's a mass break-out. I been runnin' into Apaches for days. Thought it was the same bunch, follow' me, but it ain't! It's a whole lot of bands. What's happenin'?'

The force had topped out, now, on the west side of the mesa, and was following the deeply cut trail which would bring them out to the north and within striking distance of the fort.

Sorensen turned in his saddle to look back down the line to where the self-styled deputies were eating dust at the rear.

'I'll bet a year's pay those two know,' he said musingly. 'Best keep a sharp eye on 'em!' He looked at Cassidy sharply.

'Best scout on ahead and see what we're riding into, Cass,' he said. 'Want a trooper with you?'

Cassidy shook his head, and shot a glance at Sarah who was riding behind with the sergeant, whose eyes never left the landscape either side of the trail, but who was plainly delighted with her company.

'No, I'm best alone,' he said. 'You hear shootin' come a-runnin' though! I'll likely need you!'

He clucked at the horse, and loped on ahead of the column.

CHAPTER TWELVE

Cassidy pushed on as fast as he could without raising a dust cloud, and was not very surprised when he came across some drag marks down the centre of the exposed ground.

A few hundred yards further up, there were two packages of brushwood lying in the trail. He could even pick out the hoofprints where they had left the brushwood and headed for a notch in the mesa rim.

He made a mental note of the notch for future reference.

But hardly had he turned the corner of an overhanging rock than his horse pricked up its ears and turned its head sideways to listen to its own back trail. Cassidy had heard nothing himself, but he was too experienced to ignore the beast's hints, and he turned off behind the next rock, took his rifle and scrambled up the rock to see back down the way he had just come.

Sarah, jogging along, rifle in hand, waved the weapon at him cheerfully and spurred her mount forward to round the rock. He slid down and walked to meet her.

'Hello, there! You forgot me!' she said accusingly. 'I had to ride hard to catch up!'

He looked back down her back trail and swore to himself as he saw the dust hanging in the air. All his care had been in vain. A blind Indian with a bad head cold would not miss the signs of someone travelling fast.

'And that means the Apaches know we're here!' he said, glumly. 'We might just as well drop back on the column, now.'

Sarah grinned like a twelve year-old, all teeth and eyes.

'They know already. There are two of 'em flanking you uphill. I could see them as I came up from the column,' she said flatly. 'These Indians are just as bright as the Afghans!'

This was so true, that he gave up trying to tell her off, and started planning their next move. If there were Indians between them and the column Sorensen had to know, and he had to keep himself and Sarah out of their hands.

Cassidy solved the problem of warning the column simply by firing three spaced shots into the air. The reports echoed back from the rocks, and must have been easily audible to anybody within twenty miles, echoing back from the towering heights above them.

'Very effective!' said Sarah uneasily, surveying the countryside for signs of life. 'Now they know we are here, and they can come and get us when they like.'

Cassidy nodded. 'And Sorensen knows it, which he didn't afore,' he pointed out, shortly. He was still uneasy. Somewhere there were at least two Apache warriors, and maybe more, and they would be watching him and Sarah and making their plans, none of which would include his or Sarah's continued good health.

'Where was them two Apaches when you last saw 'em?' he asked.

'Back there a little way. I didn't actually know they were stalking you. They seemed to be looking up the side of the mountain, here.'

'And they didn't see you?'

'Not so far as I could make out. Funny, really, I wasn't hidden, but they just didn't look my way, I suppose.'

'Or they was after somebody else?'

'That's possible, too,' she agreed equably.

But who? Or were they looking for the warriors from the far side of the mesa coming down to join them? They must know by now that their ambush had failed. He was thinking about it when the cavalry came into sight, moving cautiously but making good time. Sorensen stopped the column when he saw Cassidy and the girl, and gave a gusty sigh of relief.

'Ma'am, when you decide to take off on your own, I'd sure appreciate it if you'd let me know! Come to that, I'd appreciate it if you didn't go off on your own, when we're facing Apache attack!'

'Certainly, Captain,' she said demurely. 'I suppose I just wasn't thinking. Silly old me!'

Sorensen's expression said much more loudly than words what he thought of the apology, which indicated to Cassidy that the soldier was learning about Lady Sarah as fast as Cassidy.

The scout checked and could see the two self-styled lawmen still tagged on to the end of the column though they looked ill at ease, and looked behind them often.

Admittedly, it was a situation to make anybody nervous but they seemed even more so than the rest of the column. He came to a sudden decision.

'Captain Sorensen, I'd like to ask them two *hombres* as tagged on with you a few questions,' he said formally. 'Mind if I do it here? There's enough cover against the uphill slope so the Apaches can't surprise us from above, and they can't get at us from below without exposin' themselves on the slope.'

'Ask away,' Sorensen agreed. 'I'll be interested in the answers myself!'

Curry and Tranter watched them approach with visible unease, and Cassidy was pretty certain that only the fear of the Apache kept them from running for it.

Within minutes, they wished they had, whatever the risks.

'Turn out your saddle-bags,' Cassidy said without any preamble. 'Put them on that rock over there! Do it now!'

As he spoke his eye was caught by a little rush of small stones and sand from the middle of the apparently empty slope of the mesa above their position.

'Keep your head down, Cap,' he said under his breath. 'We ain't alone!'

Neither of what he was now certain were fake lawmen seemed to have noticed the little landslide. After a few mumbled protests they started to unload their saddle-bags. The tail end scouts caught up with the column, and blocked their escape in any case, and the eyes of a lot of the soldiers nearest to the rock were fascinated.

O'Rourke growled at them to keep a good lookout, and their attention snapped back to the hillside. There was another little avalanche of debris, and a number of carbine muzzles drifted over to cover it.

'Reckon we got Indians up there, Cass?' said O'Rourke, in a low voice.

'Certain sure!' Cassidy agreed. 'But if it's them shiftin' that sand, they don't care if we know. Apache'll cross a snowdrift without makin' footprints iffen he's a mind to!'

O'Rourke said suddenly: 'If your hand comes outa that there bag with anything in it, you can stop worryin' about the Apaches, Trant. I'll kill you meself!'

The double click of his Colt coming to full cock sounded loud in the still mountain air, and Tranter, whose arm had been plunged to the bottom of his saddle-bag, drew his hand very slowly into sight. It was empty.

O'Rourke reached out and took the bag, and upended it on the flat rock. From it tumbled a revolver and a knotted bandanna which chinked when it hit the stone. Tranter could not stop himself starting to make a grab for it, but O'Rourke's gun butt smashed on to the back of his hand.

'You!' Cassidy pointed at Curry. 'Empty his other bag.'

Curry was white and his hand was trembling, and he had to make two tries at picking it up. Death was very close in the still, hot air, and Cassidy checked the mountainside above and below them. The Indians were there, he knew, but why had they not already attacked?

Out of the saddle-bag came another bandanna and Sorensen pulled off his gauntlets and began picking at the knot of the first one. It came open immediately, and a variety of jewellery tumbled out. It was all heavy work, made of silver and set with opaque red and blue stones. The work on the bracelets was intricate and in the middle of the wrist of each was a large, hooked, black claw polished to a high shine and held in a solid silver setting.

There were a couple of necklaces in the shape of the flowers which bloomed on squash plant, and a belt of heavy silver plates linked with silver rings.

'Didn't get those off no Apaches,' said Cassidy, positively. 'That there's Navajo work. Good quality, too. And there's a Hopi buckle on that there belt. Can't mistake it. Some come off warriors, all right. But those there are worn by women.

'And that one' – he picked up a small bracelet lovely in its silverwork – 'that's a child's first bracelet!'

'We ... found them!' said Curry desperately. 'Took 'em off an Apache been raidin' north, I reckon.'

'But I thought you just came up from Tucson via Phoenix?' said Sorensen. 'You haven't had time to get involved with Apaches. Have you?'

Before either of the men could reply, there was a spatter of firing from up the slope, and a shrill yell of triumph. The Apaches had arrived from their frustrated ambush on the far side of the ridge.

At the very first shot, the cavalrymen were off their horses and lying flat on the hillside, rifles searching for targets. One or two fired, but their language said they had missed and knew they had missed. Sarah, peering through her telescopic sight, fired, and an Apache who had been moving to outflank the column threw up his arms and fell to roll bonelessly down the hill.

A trooper along the road watched Sarah reload with interest and turned his head to find Cassidy watching him in turn.

'That is one helluva lot o' woman, Cass,' he said in a respectful voice. 'Sure you can handle 'er?'

'Think I want to lose an arm?' Cassidy – who was equally impressed though not as surprised – replied, with feeling. 'You should've seen her deal with a charge!'

A shot raised a tiny fountain of dust near his face and suddenly they were busy again, a hail of bullets and stone splinters flying about their refuge.

His hearing dulled by the reports of the rifles to either side of him, Cassidy did not at first notice that the volume of firing had suddenly doubled until the tones of a bugle cut through the din.

Amazed, he ducked below the edge of the path, and looked around. He could feel through the rock the dull thunder of approaching cavalry, but the spatter of new rifle fire was closer.

He took a cautious look up the slope, to see a dusty form scurrying along the hillside and away from the approaching horses. The troopers along the road were holding their fire as the Apaches made off along the side of the butte, and disappeared.

Round the side of the butte a column of troopers appeared, the lead men firing after the disappearing Indians until the man at the head of the column, a bearded figure in civilian clothes, riding on a mule, raised his hand and an officer barked an order.

'Who on earth is that?' asked Sarah in a stage whisper.

'General Crook,' Cassidy told her tersely. 'Finest Indian fighter I ever did see, and the canniest. Knows Apaches better than any of those lunkheads in Washington. If anybody can end these damned Indian wars, he can!'

General Crook watched as the officers deployed their men, and called Sorensen to him. The captain walked up the trail, beckoning to Sarah and Cassidy as he went. Cassidy, getting up from his position in the dust, dusted himself down, then glanced down at himself, and realized how ludicrous was the gesture in his scarecrow clothes.

Crook ran a frosty eye over him, glanced at Sarah and snorted.

'How come every time I see you, Cassidy, your look less like a soldier and more like a saddle tramp?' he snapped.

'People keep shootin' at me, General,' Cassidy said equably. 'Can't get 'em to stop!'

Crook snorted, but he turned his attention to Sarah without more comment, and teeth gleamed on his thick beard. Cassidy realized with a start that the general was smiling, down there in the undergrowth.

'Lady Sarah, I presume ! It's a relief to find you unhurt, ma'am! I trust my men have given you no cause for complaint?'

Sarah grinned like a schoolgirl. 'They saved my life, General,' she said. 'It would be a graceless woman who complained about the men who did that – and the one who saved it more often than anybody else is Mr Cassidy, here.'

The general's beard twitched, and he shot a sharp look at Cassidy.

'Nothing wrong with his manners, anyway!' he snorted. 'Sergeant!'

The NCO sat sharply upright and saluted. 'Got a spare shirt and breeches on one of the mules?' asked Crook.

'Yessir!'

'Give 'em to Cassidy and let him get decently dressed!' He pointed a finger like a field gun at the scout. 'And then you can explain to me why half the law in Arizona Territory seems to think you are the worst thing to happen since Geronimo took to the hills!'

CHAPTER THIRTEEN

General George Crook might have been the finest Indian fighter of his generation, but he was certainly not a dedicated killer of Indians. When off his mule, he looked more like a successful businessman with a taste for opera and Sunday-go-to-chapel manners.

He rarely wore a uniform, even in the field, rode a mule instead of a horse, and carried a shotgun instead of a rifle. It was more use at short range and a charge of buckshot deters even the most belligerent Indian, he pointed out. In fact, he believed that if the Government of the United States were to work with the Indians instead of against them, they would become more easily pacified.

He led the column down from the mesa and

into a clearing in the trees where a running stream turned the air cool and there was room for the whole of his command to rest in safety, set sentries, sent his animals to be watered, and had blankets spread on the ground. An orderly produced a folding table and laid it in front of him.

Courtly and polite, he seated Sarah on a blanket on a natural armchair in the rocks, handed her coffee and had water brought for her to wash off the dust of the trail.

Then he turned eyes like gun-barrels on Cassidy and barked: 'Come here, man, and report! You seem to have turned the whole of the basin into a boiling cauldron of trouble, and I have to bring out a whole mountain battery and half of my command to settle it down! Why?'

Cassidy, who had been shouted at by field marshals with less effect, blinked rapidly and forced himself not to spring, quivering, to attention.

'Well, now, General,' he began, and saw Crook's brows begin to gather. 'Wasn't me got 'em riled up. Not like this! Started when I was coming down from Chico, up beyond.'

'I want a report, not your life story!' growled Crook ominously. 'Get on with it!'

'Sure, General, I'm just getting' to it! I started

out down here to chase some *hombres* held up the bank in Chico, and took my money along with everybody else's.'

There was an ominous rumble from the general.

'I seen the tracks of them as hit the bank, and I wasn't about to let my life's savin's go off down the mountain. There's some of my blood on them dollars, and I wanted it back!'

'The Indians, man, get on with the Indians!'

'Yeah,' said Cassidy. 'I'm just comin' to them, General.'

Crook waved a hand at him, and drank from his mug of coffee. Cassidy watched his beard bob at every swallow, and yearned.

'Well, soon as I hit the Rim I ran into trouble. Last time I was down this way, the Tonto Apaches wasn't friendly. But they wasn't on the prod, neither.

'But for days, me and Lady Sarah been runnin' and hidin'! At first I thought it was just the one war party real mad, then I realized it was more'n one, and more'n mad. Somethin' or someone got the Indians riled up, and they blame all white men for it.'

Another growl from the luxurious beard. Cassidy could tell he was telling the general nothing he did not already know.

'Well, General, I seen Tontos, Chiricahua, Jicarilla and some I ain't even worked out yet. Most of 'em should be miles away from here, but they ain't! Sergeant O'Rourke!'

The sergeant had been hovering around away from the general's line of sight, and stepped forward smartly, snapped off a salute which almost crackled, and dumped on the improvised table the bundles of jewellery taken from the two fake marshals. They made a considerable pile.

Crook examined them carefully, and his face darkened when he came across the tiny, baby-sized bracelet. He turned it over in his fingers, and glanced around.

'Bring those two marshals here,' he ordered when Cassidy had explained about the jewellery. 'I want to hear what they have to say.'

But the marshals had disappeared somewhere between the trail and the woods. The troopers in charge of watering the horses, when questioned, said they thought the marshals had been seen watering their own horses a little further downstream. But when a search was mounted, there was nothing to be found except the tracks of two horses angling away through the woods. They were gone.

'They will not get far in these woods without the

protection of the troopers,' Crook opined, sourly. 'But the Apache will not know they are operating without our approval. They have undone in a few months the work I have been doing for the whole of my tour of duty!'

He jabbed a finger at Cassidy.

'You are a tracker, Cassidy! Track them! Bring them back if you can and kill them if you cannot!'

He caught O'Rourke's eye on him, and coughed.

'Ahem! That is, of course, if every effort to bring them back alive has been made and found to fail!'

He stopped, leaned forward and beckoned Cassidy to the table. When the scout bent forward to listen carefully, the general dropped his voice.

'Either way, stop them doing any more harm. They have to be stopped and that right now!'

Cassidy nodded. 'I'll do my best, sir!' he said, his mind full of Apaches who had no way of distinguishing him from the fugitives and who would not mind much either way, anyway. At least, he thought, Sarah would be safe.

Back on his mount, clad in US Cavalry breeches and dark blue shirt, with his Winchester riding the saddle horn, and a full canteen and biscuit bag slung on the horn, and enough ammunition to start a war, he trotted off into the woods.

The ponderosa pines crowded close around him as he took up the trail, waving shade over him as he went and cutting down the heat of the sun. The two fake marshals were not hard to track. They had been too eager to put ground between themselves and the Army to be careful. Overturned needles left darker patches in the ground cover, and occasionally, a horse had brushed against the end of a branch and left hairs there to tell the tale.

The stones which had been overturned were still dark underneath, proving the men had passed recently. In this heat damp left by the morning dew evaporated quickly.

Like his quarry, Cassidy made good time, hardly breaking his horse's stride. He kept a sharp lookout to the sides where a tracking Indian would ride, but saw no suspicious signs. On this trail at any rate, the bandits were not being followed except by Cassidy.

At the back of his mind, there was still a faint surprise that Sarah had accepted his instructions to stay with Crook where she would be safe, rather than coming with him. She had merely nodded demurely and said: 'Yes, Mr Cassidy!'

It was not like Sarah, and obscurely he missed her. He had been getting used to having his back guarded by a good shot.

But what could he expect? A woman naturally stayed close to the dominant male, and Crook was about as dominant as males get. Cassidy shook off the thought, and concentrated on not getting killed while tracking two murderers through country seething with natural born killers.

It took a lot of his attention, and when he suddenly caught up with the fugitives, he almost overran them in his haste.

The trees fell back over a low dome of bedrocks, making a clearing with a stone floor littered with rocks.

Curry and Tranter were about halfway across it, travelling slowly, and he could see that Tranter's horse was limping. As he watched, the man swung down, lifted the animal's hoof and examined it briefly. Then he let go of it, and shook his head. Curry had not dismounted, and he did not offer to do so. Instead, he raised himself in his stirrups and looked carefully around the edges of the open ground. It the shade of the trees, Cassidy apparently went unnoticed.

The two men were discussing something between themselves and the discussion was becoming heated. Cassidy could imagine the trend of their conversation.

Tranter was trying to persuade Curry to let him ride double, and Curry was not prepared to risk himself and his own chances of escape by exhausting the horse. Cassidy could see his head being shaken more and more emphatically. At the same time, he was backing away from Tranter, his horse stepping awkwardly on the rock.

Tranter made a violent gesture, turned back to his lamed animal, and mounted it, drawing his rifle from the saddle boot. He forced the limping horse after Curry across the clearing, trying to catch him up, but the other man's horse was gaining on him at an easy lope, and it was clear Tranter was not going to catch him.

Suddenly, the trailing man jammed the rifle to his shoulder and fired at his comrade's receding back. Whether or not the shot went anywhere near Curry was not clear, but it certainly did not bring him off his horse, which went off like a frightened rabbit, in a series of convulsive leaps.

Tranter fired again, and a third time, but the target was receding and its motion erratic. Cassidy could see the bullet raising puffs of stone from the ground, then realized other shooters had joined in.

The Apaches came out of the trees on the opposite side of the stone pan, riding like centaurs and shooting as they came. Curry dragged his horse round sharply and began coming back at a hard gallop.

As he came, he passed Tranter, who was shouting to him, presumably begging for a ride. The man tried to spur his own limping mount into a gallop, and the animal tried valiantly to obey, but its hurt leg let it down, and it fell.

Tranter was pitched out of the saddle on to the rock. Thrown on to the bare rock, he dropped his rifle and climbed to his feet, one arm dangling.

The Apaches were almost upon him as he pulled his pistol from its holster and began firing at the nearest ones, either to drive them towards his fleeing comrade, or to try and secure himself a replacement mount. Either way, he was unsuccessful. Leaving their comrades to pursue the fleeing Curry, two warriors rode round Tranter, and began circling him, whooping and waving at him derisively.

Tranter threw himself down behind his fallen horse, firing at the circling warriors with his pistol, but an Apache was as capable as anybody else of counting bullets expended. Their name for a handgun was a 'shoots six', and they were aware that white men often left the chamber under the hammer empty to avoid accidental discharge so they simply slung themselves on the opposite side of their mounts, and waited for the sixth – or maybe fifth – shot.

The sixth was not long in coming, and the Indians immediately rushed the fallen horse from both sides. The Colt revolver had one defect in that each empty cartridge had to be poked out of its chamber individually and the empty chamber reloaded the same way.

The renegade simply did not have time even to empty the cylinder before the Apaches were upon him. Cassidy saw the warriors leap from their horses, and fall upon the outlaw. After a brief struggle, the activity stopped and the scout saw that they had captured Tranter alive. The man's fate in their hands was sickening to contemplate, but Cassidy remembered the very small bracelet in the bandits' treasure sack, and his mouth set in a hard, merciless line.

'As ye sow . . .' he murmured to himself, and turned his horse to follow after Curry.

The man was not hard to find. He was holed up on top of a rocky outcrop, his horse's corpse laid like a discarded sack nearby, and his rifle poking out from the mound of boulders to mark his hiding place.

Once again there was little Cassidy could do

about it. The Indians were between him and his quarry, and in any case outnumbered him. He had no intention of throwing his life away for a murderous bandit.

He was just preparing to slip back through the woods and return to the general when there was the flat slap of different kind of rifle, and one of the attacking Apaches threw up his arms and fell sideways to the ground. The first shot was followed by three more in quick succession, one of which found a mark and seemed to come from a different direction.

The Apaches came to the same conclusion as Cassidy, and took to their heels. From his rock pile, Curry dusted two more as they fled, and the woods fell silent. One of the downed warriors suddenly sprang to his feet and ran, jinking like a fleeing hare, into the trees. His derisive cries as he went out of range presumably made him feel better about losing his horse, but being dismounted to a man used from birth to travelling long distances at speed and with virtually no supplies was not as terrible a prospect as it was to a white man.

There was a moment's silence, and then Curry's voice called from the rock pile.

'Who's there?' he shouted.

There was a silence. Nobody replied, and he

called again and again. Then: 'I'm comin' out! Don't shoot!'

He appeared, holding his rifle above his head, and scrambled down the rock pile, to where his horse was lying. One of the Indian ponies lay close to it, and the body of one of the warriors was half buried under it. Curry stopped to make sure the man was dead, then pulled out his knife and bent over the corpse.

As he did so, a familiar figure emerged from the trees at the other side of the rock pile, and Cassidy groaned to recognize Sarah, walking with her rifle at the trail and leading a horse.

She came up on Curry just as he stood, a hank of black hair still dripping blood over his left hand, and stepped away from the corpse.

Sarah stopped, shocked.

'Oh, botheration take it!' she said disgustedly. 'I thought you were—'

'Thought I was who?' Curry was grinning. 'General Crook? Naw, lady, I ain't one of them guys. But you still look pretty good to me, with everything I need just right at this moment! I need a horse, and you bring me one. I need more ammunition, and you bring me some o' that, too!

'And just right at this moment, I could do with some female companionship – killin' Indians always makes me kinda horny! So before I go on my way, you can do me a load o' good, and maybe I won't kill you before I go!'

Sarah was caught with both arms immobilized, and no way to get her rifle into action before the gunman could cut her down, and though every line of her body betrayed taut rage, she had no choice but to stand still.

As bad luck would have it, she had stopped exactly between Cassidy and Curry, and her horse blocked a shot from one side while her body masked the gunman from the other.

Cassidy swung on to his horse to move his position, but Curry, his attention on the girl, did not notice him.

'Come on, girl!' he was saying. 'Ground hitch that horse, and drop the cannon. I can kill you before you even get it into line, anyway. Time for you to find out what a real man's like! I'll—'

He suddenly realized that Cassidy was looking over the girl's shoulder, and read his death in the scout's eyes. Desperately, he grabbed for his Colt.

'Wrong!' said Cassidy flatly, and the report of his Winchester was loud in the clearing.

Between Curry's eyes a hole appeared, and blood and brains sprayed out of the back of his head. For a second, his reflexes carried on the movement which would have brought his pistol into his hand and to aim. Then his legs collapsed and he crumpled like a puppet with its strings cut.

'What the hangment do you think you're doing here?' Cassidy exploded at the girl. 'I left you safe with Crook! What in tarnation's name. . . ?'

'I was worried about you,' she said crossly. 'You have a genius for getting yourself into trouble when I'm not with you!'

Her face began to crumple prettily, and Cassidy had her in his arms and his lips were on hers before it occurred to him that he had not actually seen any tears in those remarkable eyes.

She disengaged her lips and laid her head against his chest, then gave a surprisingly girlish giggle.

'I can hear your heart going like a steam train!' she told him, and straightened up to look him in the eye.

'Now, Cassidy, where exactly is this ranch of ours? The Superstitions, did you say?'

Cassidy, who had thought he was getting himself out of trouble, began to suspect his real problems were only just beginning.

'Now, see here. . . .' he started.

'You are going to like my father. He's a soldier, too. He's also about five thousand miles way in

England, so we won't need to worry about him interfering. We'll be married by the time he can get here!' she said.

And they were.